ALANA'S LIST

BY

C. DEANNE ROWE

ALANA'S LIST
by C. Deanne Rowe

Published by Citrine Group, L.L.C.
Des Moines, IA

Cover Creation by Rebecca K. Sterling, Sterling Design Studios

First Printing: January 2021

ISBN-10: 978-1-946122-30-8
ISBN-13/EAN-13: 978-1-946122-30-8

Printed in the United States of America

DEDICATION

Alana's list is dedicated to all those looking for love. It will find you when you're not looking for it.

PROLOGUE

"What is wrong with men?" Sinking down on the couch next to her grandmother, Alana Andrews let out a huge sigh.

"You're home early. It sounds like tonight didn't go well." Her grandmother lowered the volume on the television, glanced at her watch as she turned to face Alana.

"It was awful. I don't remember the last time I've been so disgusted with a guy." Alana put her arms down to her side, pushed her head back against the couch and let out a sound of angst.

"Tell me what happened."

Alana knew her grandmother would understand how she felt. She was the one who always quizzed Alana about the boys she liked since she was a little girl. There were tons of questions about how they treated her, if they made her laugh, if they gave her all of their attention when other people were around.

Alana still remembered the day she came home from kindergarten excited because a boy in her class she really liked paid attention to her. She couldn't wait to tell her mother and grandmother about everything that happened. Her grandmother stopped her when Alana mentioned she had shared her candy with the boy. Her grandmother stopped her to ask if he had shared candy with her. Alana was so crazy about this boy it didn't matter to her. She was so happy he talked to her and sat by her at lunch. Her grandmother wasted no time setting her straight on how she was to be treated by a boy and that didn't include him not sharing his candy with her. She deserved better than that.

"If you watch, your grandfather always shares his candy with me. Make sure whoever it is you fall in love with shares his candy with you. Even if it's his last piece."

Alana still noticed the gleam in her grandmother's eyes when her she talked about her grandfather. It always made her smile.

"He was on his phone all night. One call after the other. It was like he didn't care if I was there." Alana adjusted her position on the couch. "Then when we met up with the friends who had been calling him, he didn't have anything to say to me. He spent the rest of the evening joking around with them. Of course, when he dropped me off just now, he was very interested in me."

"He sounds like a winner."

"He acted like he was a winner. Don't worry though. I knocked him down a few notches before I got out of the car. I don't think I have to worry about him asking me out again." Alana watched her grandmother put a hand over her mouth to try and cover the smile on her face. "Please tell me how you knew grandpa was the one for you."

"He met all the qualities on my list."

"Your list? You had a list?" Alana laughed.

"Of course. Every guy I dated had to meet those qualities or I never dated them again."

"Every one of them?" Alana asked. "You mean there wasn't one thing on your list Grandpa didn't met?"

"Well, there was dancing." Her grandmother smiled as she shook her head.

"Dancing? That was the only quality Grandpa didn't have you thought was important?" Alana watched her grandmother stare off into the distance for a few seconds. The smile on her face grew larger.

"Yes. That was the only quality your grandfather didn't have. Of course, over the years I tried to teach him how to dance but he just had no rhythm." Her grandmother laughed and then put her hand on Alana's. "Your grandfather was a good man. He wasn't perfect but he was honest, trustworthy, patient, and oh how he could make me laugh. He was my best friend."

Alana watched the expression on her grandmother's face go from seriousness to happiness with a twinge of sadness mixed in as the memories of her husband ran through her mind. Alana could tell she missed him and was lonely even after her parents moved her in with them. She knew it wasn't the same. Alana tried to spend as much time with her as she could. It was her way of keeping her grandfather's memory alive because she missed him also.

"Will you do me a favor, Grandma?" Alana stood up from the couch.

"Anything dear."

"Will you write that list of qualities down for me. I want to make sure when *I* meet the person I'm meant to spend my life with, I'll know it. Oh, and add dancing. I'm sure Grandpa won't mind." She reached out her hands for her grandmother to take. "Let's dance."

Her grandmother grasped Alana's hands as she stood from the couch, a huge smile on her face. Alana took her cell from her jeans pocket, found one of her favorite songs and turned up the volume.

CHAPTER ONE

Ten years later

With one big sweep of her hand, Alana Andrews cleared the corner of her bathroom counter of any reminder of him. A few bottles of cologne, his deodorant, and hairbrush all fell into the empty trash bag. Opening the top drawer of the vanity, she tossed his toothbrush and toothpaste in as well.

Next was the closet. Hangers and all went into another bag which was headed for the closest donation bin. A fresh start was what she needed. Almost two years of her life wasted. Alana felt a tugging in her chest which always occurred when she faced what happened. Maybe she shouldn't consider the past two years a waste. She did learn she would never let another man into her life or her heart again so easily. Her grandmother had tried to prepare her to find the right person. This time she must have been blind.

She was positive he was the one she'd share her life with. He had every one of the required traits on her grandmother's list. Or did he? Maybe she glossed over a few of those traits hoping John would eventually develop them. *What were you thinking Alana?*

Her grandmother hadn't told her how to deal with the heartbreak when her list wasn't enough. Alana couldn't count on her mother for inspiration. She and her father had their share of problems and finally divorced after Alana left for college. How they managed to stay together that long was somewhat of a miracle.

How could John leave her and for another woman? Not just another woman…her best friend. Betrayed by the two people closest to her. How could she not see what was going on? Did her feelings for him cause her to be totally oblivious to the way he acted around Kim? Thinking back there were clues. Ones she should have picked up on but chose to ignore.

"Never again!" She exclaimed as she dropped the last of his shirts into the bag. She spread all of her hanging blouses and slacks out on the rod to cover the empty space, then placed the bag by the door.

Wiping away a falling tear, she took another look around the room to make sure there was nothing else to remind her of him. Alana spotted the pillow on her bed. The one that still had a faint remainder of his scent. The one she cried herself to sleep on for the first few weeks after he left.

"Oh, that has to go for sure." Alana picked up the pillow and tossed it against the bag of clothes. "As soon as these are dropped off in the donation bin, every last sign of him will be gone from the bedroom. Good riddance. Now for the rest of the apartment."

Walking through each room one more time, Alana looked for anything else that might remind her of him. She realized she couldn't toss out the furniture. That was a little unrealistic. She *could* get rid of his video game console though. The one she bought him for Christmas last year. The one he spent more time playing than he spent with her. She'd feel so much better if it went to some child who would enjoy it.

"That goes also." Alana unhooked the console from her television, loading it along with any games in an empty box. "Now the kitchen."

A few mugs he always drank coffee from, one she bought him for his birthday which said *Best Boyfriend Ever,* went in the box along with a beer mug he kept in the freezer because he couldn't drink from a can. That should have been a huge clue.

She made one last pass through her apartment to make sure she didn't miss anything. Satisfied she had cleared out everything memories of him were attached to, she picked up the bags and box then walked out to her car.

Loading the trunk of her car with all she collected from her apartment, she checked to make sure there was nothing inside the car she needed to throw away. She was always the one driving when they would go anywhere. Not only did he cheat on her, but he was cheap. It was her apartment he'd moved into, and only occasionally paid part of the rent. She paid for the gas and most of the time their meals as well. How could she be so stupid?

"Never again!" Alana slammed the lid of her trunk.

As she got closer to the donation center, Alana spotted a scruffy man walking down the road in her direction. He was pushing a shopping cart that looked to be filled with everything he owned.

From what she could tell through the layers of clothing he wore; he would be about the same height and size as John. Pulling over to the side of the road, she lowered her passenger window and waited until the man was close enough to hear her.

"Excuse me, sir."

"Me?" The gentleman put his hand on his chest looking a little confused.

"Yes, you," Alana replied. "I was going to take some men's clothes to the donation center. They look like they would fit you. Would you like to have them instead of me donating them? There are some very nice shirts."

"If you're giving them away. I can't afford to pay you for them." The gentleman put his hands in his pants pockets and turned the lining inside out.

"You don't have to pay me," she called out the window. "I'm giving them to you, if you want them. I would rather see you have them. That way the donation center doesn't have to tag them and have them take up space on their racks in the store. Better yet, they won't cost you a dime."

"Yes, I'll take them. I can always use some new clothes." The gentleman ran his hands down the worn clothing he was wearing.

"Wait right there." Alana checked the traffic, popped her trunk lid and opened her car door. She grabbed the bags then the box and walked toward the gentleman. As she reached his shopping cart, she placed the bags and box on top of everything else in his cart.

"Wow. I don't know what to say." The gentleman seemed surprised by how full the bags were. He picked up one of the coffee mugs and smiled.

"You don't have to say anything. Wear them proudly. Enjoy the gaming system; give it away or sell it. I don't care." Alana held her finger in the air. "Oh, and promise me you won't leave your girlfriend for her best friend."

The gentleman looked confused as he began untying the bag. "I promise."

"I hope you enjoy everything." Alana smiled as she made her way back to her car. Closing her car door, she took one last look at the man and noticed the huge smile on his face as he pulled a few of the shirts from the bag and held them close to his body. Finally, she felt closure. John was gone from her life for good.

CHAPTER TWO

"I'm telling you it felt so liberating." Alana looked
around the cafeteria for somewhere to sit, Carter Owens
following close behind. She placed her sandwich down
on the table in the corner of the room and then sat in
one of the chairs. "Thanks for meeting me for lunch,
Carter. I know the cafeteria isn't the best place to have
lunch, but it's close for both of us." She'd worked at
Talley and Jones Law Firm as a paralegal for five years
but normally ate at her desk even though they provided
a lunch room with a scenic view of downtown Houston.

"It's a lot fancier than the one in my building. I
went to work for the government for the job security not
the fringe benefits. Besides it's nice to get out of there
for a little while and I want to hear more about your
cleansing experience." Carter laughed as he took a seat
across from Alana at the table.

"I can't tell you how long I've been meaning to get rid of all his stuff and now I did." Alana leaned in and smiled. "Watching that man's face as he looked through the bags and box made it even more satisfying."

Alana glanced across the table at Carter. The times she and John had joined him and Kim for dinner, he'd wear tight jeans, his shirt tucked in, with a cowboy hat and boots on. Today he was dressed for work, dress slacks and shirt, so he blended into the downtown Houston work crowd but still kept his western twist with his cowboy boots. Apparently, the Department of Agriculture allowed them to dress a little more casually than most. From what she understood about his career he sat behind a desk making contacts by phone or email and writing reports. She had even listened to a few of the market reports he gave over the radio. She guessed that didn't require a suit and tie.

"I would have given them to you but you have a few more muscles than John and you're into the cowboy look. Totally different styles."

"You're right about that." Carter pointed to his cowboy boots under the table. "I don't think his stuff would have worked for me. It looked good on him, but not for me. It's good news though. It helped me when I cleaned all of Kim's stuff from my apartment. I'm glad you finally took that step."

"Me too. *I'm* glad you kept suggesting it to me." Alana lifted the top piece of bread and checked her sandwich to make sure there were no onions anywhere to be found.

"Did they leave the onions off this time?" Carter laughed as he leaned in pretending to inspect her sandwich himself.

"Yes, they did. I swear John would make sure and order my stuff with onions just to piss me off." Alana noticed the smile on Carter's face. "You don't believe me?"

"I wouldn't put it past him to do something like that. He was a piece of work." Carter shook his head as she straightened the lettuce on her sandwich.

"Me either. He could be a real ass most of the time. I can't believe I put up with him for as long as I did." Alana took a bite of her sandwich.

"Well now he's Kim's problem. I think she likes onions though." Carter leaned back as he waited for Alana to try and land her hand on his arm or wherever she could reach. "I can't believe they played us both. I would've never guessed she was fooling around with John. Those texts you found on John's phone really took me by surprise."

"Me too, but you're right. They did play us both. I guess that either makes us both fools or lucky."

"Lucky?" Carter asked almost choking on the bite of sandwich he took.

"Yeah, lucky. They're out of our lives and they deserve each other, onions and all." Carter's laugh made Alana smile. Something she hadn't been doing a lot of lately.

"I agree with that, but I certainly didn't feel lucky when I found out from you they were messing around behind our backs." Carter took another bite of his sandwich.

"I'm sorry I had to be the one to tell you, but I hope if the tables had been turned, you would've told me." Alana watched his expression to see if he agreed.

"Of course, I would've. I know it had to be hard on you though." Carter sat back in his chair. "He was your boyfriend and she was your best friend. It was a double whammy for you."

"You're right, but it wasn't easy for either of us. I'm just glad we made it through and can still say we're friends. That's one good thing that came out of it. We're a couple of sad twenty-somethings trying to make each other feel better." Alana moved her sandwich around on her plate. Thinking about what happened brought back all those feelings she'd been trying to forget.

"I promise if I start dating again, and that's a big if, I won't introduce her to your boyfriend if you have one by then." Carter pointed his finger in her direction.

"Deal." Alana smiled. "It's a big if that I'll ever date again either."

"Oh yes you will. There's some guy out there just waiting for you. You'll know it when you meet him." Carter nodded.

"I thought that about John. I think I'll just adopt a few cats and be a spinster." Alana let another smile cross her face.

"Cats?" Carter asked.

"Yeah. Two, three or ten. That should be enough." Alana shrugged one shoulder.

"Man, that'll be stinky." Carter scrunched up his nose. "I thought growing up on a farm smelled sometimes, but cats. That's a completely different story."

"I would adopt dogs, but then I'd have to walk them and when I get too old, I'll have to hire someone to walk them and it'll probably be a young, handsome, studly man. It's a vicious circle." Alana took another bite of her sandwich and sighed.

"Cats it is." Carter grinned as he stood from the table. "I've got to get back to work. I've got a big project I'm working on. It was good to see you and I'm happy you finally got rid of your extra baggage. I'm proud of you." Carter leaned down and gave her a quick hug. "Keep in touch."

"Thanks, Carter." Alana watched as Carter walked out the door of the cafeteria. It felt good to have someone to talk to and vent with. He understood what she was feeling because he was probably feeling the same thing too.

As she finished her sandwich, she glanced around the room checking all the couples having lunch together, talking, laughing, smiling.

Reaching in her purse, she pulled out her wallet and unfolded a worn piece of paper her grandmother had given her years ago. It was a handwritten list of traits her grandmother felt were important in finding a partner.

Reading through the list she nodded at the ones she realized now John didn't have. They must be honest and sincere. They must have a sense of humor. They must show kindness and compassion. They must show you trust and support. And most important, they must be your best friend.

Her grandmother always insisted the person she planned to share her life with must have these traits. Alana had even made sure she included them in her prayers. Maybe she should have prayed more often and referred to this list a little sooner. Maybe she wouldn't be hurting like this now. She was so blinded by John. She had managed to convince herself he met these qualities.

Alana wondered if what she told Carter about becoming a cat lady would come true. Would she never be in a relationship again? She didn't know if she'd ever again be able to trust anyone enough to open her heart. It hurt too much to have it broken.

CHAPTER THREE

A few months later

"I can't believe I went through with it. I told them I didn't want to be set up on a date. I thought it was too soon, but they wouldn't listen." Alana took a sip then placed her wineglass back down on her kitchen island before she continued. "It had to be the most humiliating thing I've been through in a long time. We had nothing to say to each other."

"It couldn't have been that bad." Carter paused for a minute. "Well, come to think of it, maybe it was."

"You're certainly a lot of help." Alana grumbled, glancing up at her grandmother's list hanging on the fridge. "I do appreciate you coming over to let me vent. My friends don't seem to understand where I'm coming from. I know they're only trying to help. Since you and I have a similar experience, I know you can relate. I'm glad we've stayed friends." Alana noticed Carter's almost empty bottle of beer. "Can I get you another beer?"

"Yes, please." Carter picked up the bottle and downed the rest.

Alana took a beer out of the refrigerator and placed the bottle in front of Carter who was sitting across the kitchen island from her. He'd arrived carrying a six-pack for himself and a bottle of her favorite white wine for her. She doubted John knew that about her.

"Anytime you need to vent, I'm your person." Carter smiled. "At least it's over now and you can move on. I'm sure your friends are through setting you up on blind dates after you told them about this guy." Carter took a drink from the new bottle.

"You would have thought so." She rolled her eyes. "When I was telling them what happened, Suzy said she met another man who she was sure was my soulmate."

"What did you tell her?" Carter folded his arms on the island and leaned forward, looking right at home.

"I told her I couldn't take anymore setups and then I pulled out the old cat lady story. I'm sure they got the hint after that."

"You're not going to become an old cat lady." Carter insisted as he shook his head.

"Sometimes I believe it would be better than going through any more dates like this one. I mean all he did was stare at his plate, play with his food, and check his phone. The man had nothing to say."

"Nothing?" Carter asked with a confused look on his face as he ran his hand over the stubble on his face.

Alana realized she liked him with a little stubble. It went nicely with his smile.

"There was an occasional yes or no or not quite sure answer." She held her hand in the air and flipped it back and forth. "If I asked him a question. Other than that, he was completely silent unless he was talking about himself. I did all the heavy lifting when it came to the conversation."

"I'm glad you like to talk or it would've been really sad." Carter chuckled.

"Hey! That was totally uncalled for." Alana tossed a half smile at him. "True, but uncalled for none the less."

"I'm joking. You know I didn't mean anything by it." Carter smiled. "All I meant was you're good at carrying the conversation. All the times the four of us spent together, you were the one who kept the conversation going."

"Apology accepted. I think." Alana gave him a questioning gaze. *What was Kim thinking when she gave up Carter for John? She had to be a fool.*

"How long was the date?" Carter attempted to change the conversation back.

"It was the longest two hours of my life. It only lasted that long because the service was so slow. Otherwise it would've been the shortest blind date in history." Alana moved around the island and took a seat on the barstool next to him.

"Was he at least nice looking?" Carter asked as he turned to face her putting the heel of his cowboy boot on the bottom rung of the barstool.

"I guess," she said as she moved around on her barstool to get comfortable.

"You guess? Didn't you see his face?" Carter watched as she got settled.

"Of course. He was nice looking, but his personality left a lot to be desired. You know me well enough to know how I am about people being attractive from the inside out."

"Yes, I do." Carter nodded. "John should have never been around as long as he was."

"You're right about that. Then you know since he was so self-absorbed it took away from his looks. To me he was a minus ten at least." Alana ran her finger down her glass of wine making a line in the moisture.

"He was ugly then." Carter smiled.

"Yes, he was. I don't do narcissistic personalities."

"That's why you and I are friends. I'm the total opposite of a narcissist. I've got such low self-esteem I've got to pull myself out of a mudhole and brush myself off every morning." Carter pretended to brush something from his shirt.

"Stop it!" She exclaimed. "You know that's not true"

"Of course, it is. Kim always made sure I knew she was much more important than me. I was so much in love I didn't see it until after she left."

"Now that's just sad," Alana pursed her lips like she was pouting.

"It is, isn't it? I'm a grown man. I should've known better. What's wrong with us?" Carter asked.

"Well, now that you know, it won't happen again." Alana reached over and patted his shoulder.

"Let's hope not. You women have a way of twisting us guys around until we don't know what's happening." Carter pretended he was twisting something between his hands. His face scrunched up on one side.

"Stop that!" Alana exclaimed as she slapped his hands. "You're right, but the right woman won't do that. She'll treat you with the respect you deserve."

"Well then, let's hope I find the right woman before I meet another Kim." He held up his bottle and she tapped it with her glass.

"Amen to that." Alana sat up straight and put her hand on Carter's arm. "Oh, I almost forgot the best part of the date."

"What's that?"

"He walked out on me and left me to pay the bill. Something about getting an emergency text from work." Alana shook her head as she watched Carter laugh so hard he almost fell off the barstool. Lifting her hand to slap him on the shoulder, she couldn't help but break into laughter herself.

CHAPTER FOUR

Glancing toward her office doorway, Alana blinked. All she could see, from the thigh down, was a muscular, hairy leg flaunting itself, trying to get her attention. Laughing, she had a good idea who the leg belonged to.

"Nice show." Alana whistled and clapped her hands. "Can I see who belongs to that gorgeous leg?"

"Good morning." Kelly's head slowly appeared in the doorway and then the rest of him followed. He walked into her office and sat on the edge of her desk. "I thought you might be bored and need some entertainment this morning."

"You're right. It was a nice break from all the paperwork I have to do today. Thank you," She nodded in acknowledgement. She enjoyed her work as a paralegal, but somedays were more hectic than others. Today was one of those days.

Kelly placed his hand on his chest and bowed. "You're welcome. Anytime I can break the monotony of your day, I'll be happy to."

"I see it's time for you to break out the shorts." Alana noticed his nicely pressed UPS uniform showing off his well-developed thighs and calves.

"It sure is. It got up to seventy-five yesterday and is supposed to be warmer today. Time to pack away the slacks." Kelly flexed his legs in front of him.

"It's a good thing you've got the legs for it." She smiled.

"Are you flirting with me?" Kelly laughed as he bent down to look under her desk checking out her feet. "It's also sandals and flip flop time for you ladies, isn't it? I love this time of the year."

Alana didn't want him staring at her feet for too long because she hadn't had a chance for a pedicure in weeks. She decided to change the conversation. "Do you have some packages for me?"

"I do. I left them on the front desk. Would you sign for them?" He handed her the stylus and the handheld computer he used to record his stops.

She signed her name and handed the computer back.

"One more thing? Would you want to go to dinner with me some night?" Kelly tilted his head sideways as he waited for her answer. "I mean, now that you are a single woman again."

"A date?" Alana was taken by surprise.

"Dinner or maybe a movie. Something relaxing and casual." He stood to leave.

Alana leaned back in her chair as she let his proposition run through her mind. He was a nice-looking man. He was a little younger than her but that really didn't matter. She knew a little about him from their previous conversations, like he'd never been married. He was a gentleman and seemed to treat her with respect when he was working.

"Why not," She replied.

Kelly flashed her a huge smile. "How about this Friday night?"

Alana watched as he picked up a post-it note pad from her desk and wrote something on it.

"Here's my cell. Text me your address and I'll pick you up around seven. How does that sound?" Kelly handed her the note.

"Perfect." Alana took the note from his hand. The expression on his face made her feel good about her decision.

****

"This is a nice place," Alana said as she followed the hostess to their table. The restaurant had a sports bar feel. There was a mixture of professionals having a beer on Friday evening and blue-collar workers enjoying time with friend so it felt comfortable. She had stayed late at work and hadn't had time to go home and change.

"Your waitress will be with you shortly." The hostess placed the menus on the table before walking away.

"Have you been here before?" Alana asked as she watched Kelly take a seat across from hers at the table. Out of his delivery uniform, he looked good in a pair of jeans and a button-down shirt. She was happy she'd accepted his offer. She looked forward to learning more about him.

"A few times," Kelly replied as the waitress approached their table with a slight grin on her face.

"What can I get you to drink?" the waitress waited for a reply without looking directly at either one of them.

"I'll take a white wine." Alana was intrigued by the expression on the waitress's face and the fact that the hostess had stopped her and said something to her before she came to their table.

"And your usual, Kelly?" the waitress asked.

"Yes. Whatever beer is on tap." Kelly quickly replied.

"I'll be right back with your drinks unless you're ready to order." The waitress waited for a reply still not looking directly at either one of them but with that strange grin on her face.

"I'd like a few more minutes please," Alana said as she watched the waitress walk away. That grin was making her curious.

"Seems like she knows you," Alana said.

"I guess I've been here more than a few times," Kelly glanced down at his menu.

"Can you give me a few suggestions on what's good then?" Alana asked. "I'm leaning toward a burger or the grilled salmon."

"If those are your two choices, I think the burgers a really good here. I've never had the salmon so I can't say for sure," Kelly said as he kept reading his menu.

"A burger it is. I'm ready to order if you are."

"I am. I'll find our waitress." Kelly looked around and then motioned for the waitress to return as soon as he spotted her.

Alana watched the waitress wave and finish the conversation she was having with the bartender. They were both staring at their table and laughing. A strange feeling grew in the pit of her stomach. She didn't like it and she wanted to know exactly what was going on.

"Ready to order?" the waitress placed a mug of beer on the table in front of Kelly and a glass of wine in front of Alana, still not looking at either of them.

"I'll take the bacon cheeseburger." Alana tried to get the waitress to look her in the eyes without any luck.

"I'll have the sirloin, medium rare with a side of fries. Please." Kelly asked.

"Oh, could you leave the onions off my burger?" Alana attempted once again to try and get the waitress to look at her.

"Sure. I can do that for you." The waitress turned and walked away.

"Since you've been here before, has our waitress waited on you?" Alana asked Kelly.

"I don't remember. Why?" Kelly asked.

"She called you by name and she seems to have an issue with looking at either of us." Alana explained.

"Maybe she has waited on me a few times. Everyone here's really friendly." Kelly quickly changed the subject. "I'm glad you agreed to go out with me. Can I ask what happened to you and your boyfriend?"

"Let's just say he liked my best friend better than me." Alana took a drink of her wine.

"That's not good." Kelly smiled. "Not good for you but good for me."

Their waitress walked toward the kitchen. Alana decided to take a chance and see if she could talk to her. Maybe the way she was acting was nothing, but she needed to know.

"I'll be right back." Alana stood from the table.

"Is everything all right?" Kelly asked.

"Everything's fine. I'll be right back." She couldn't tell Kelly what she was doing. She needed to know what the problem was with their waitress.

Catching the woman as she walked out the kitchen doors, Alana stopped her. "Hi, sorry to bother you but can I talk to you for a minute?"

"I'm a little busy." The waitress attempted to brush her off.

"I know, but I have a quick question. It'll just take a second." Alana stepped in front of her.

"Okay. What's your question?" The waitress still wouldn't look at her but her face showed she was uncomfortable.

"When you took our orders, you wouldn't look at me or the gentleman with me, yet you had this slight grin on your face. I wanted to make sure everything was all right." Alana shrugged. "Normally when I get a strange feeling, I like to find out what's going on."

"First, I wouldn't call the person at the table with you a gentleman. Second, it's got nothing to do with you." The waitress gave Alana a quick side glance.

"You do know Kelly?"

"I wish I could say I didn't but I can't." The odd little grin returned.

"Is there something about him I should know? You see I only know him from work. He delivers our UPS packages. I agreed to go on this date with him because he seems like a nice guy. Am I wrong?" Alana waited patiently for a reply.

"The only thing I can tell you is that if I were you, I would find an excuse and leave. From one woman to another, protect your feet." The waitress finally looked at her as she chuckled.

"Why would you say that?" Alana remembered the strange comment Kelly made in her office when he was inspecting her feet.

"I'm trying to be straight with you. Don't trust him and don't let him give you a foot massage. That's all I can say." The waitress attempted to walk away.

"What do you mean? Come on, you have to tell me what happened. We women have to stick together. I wouldn't let another woman be in a bad situation without doing all I could to warn her." Alana stepped in front of her and moved her hand back and forth between them to make a point as she waited for her reply.

"Fine." The waitress huffed out. "Kelly and I went out a few times. He knows that I'm on my feet at work so he offered to give me a foot massage. Seemed okay, right?"

Alana nodded in agreement.

"The man has a foot fetish." The waitress leaned in and whispered. "He gets off on women's feet. That's all I'm going to say except if I were you, I'd made an excuse not to be alone with him or if you are alone with him, don't agree to a foot massage."

The waitress walked back into the kitchen while Alana stood frozen in place. As the information sank in, she began to fell ill. She wouldn't have to make an excuse to leave. Her skin crawled at what she'd learned about Kelly. Thank goodness she had gotten caught up in a project at the office and was running late so she'd met him here. At least when she got a chance to leave, she could drive herself home. Alana was positive a foot fetish was not one of the traits on her grandmother's list.

CHAPTER FIVE

"I'm so glad you weren't busy and could walk with me to get coffee." Alana waited for Carter to make his way down the steps of his office building, his boot heels clicking on each step. He made it look so easy to walk in cowboy boots and she was beginning to like the way they looked on him.

"Sure. Anytime. I needed a break. It's such a nice day it was hard to stay chained to my desk." Carter smiled as he walked up next to her. "Tell me how your date went Friday night. I didn't hear from you all weekend so I assumed it went well," he said as they began walking down the street.

"I'm telling you it was the strangest date I've ever been on. This dating thing's not all it's cracked up to be." Alana sighed as they stopped at the corner waiting for the light to turn green so they could cross the street. She was glad she asked him to come with her. She felt comfortable talking to Carter and also being around him.

"What did you and Kelly end up doing?" Carter asked.

"We met at a sports bar that I guess he frequents because he has dated our waitress."

"I bet that was awkward." Carter smirked.

He took her hand as they stepped down off the curb, pointing down at her stilettos. "Wouldn't want you to trip."

She'd been walking in heels since high school but the feeling of her hand in his felt good so she didn't mention it. "Awkward enough that I waited for our food, took a few bites and then said I wasn't feeling well and I needed to leave." Squinting her eyes, she waited for Carter to tell her how wrong that was.

"That was a good excuse." He nodded in agreement.

"It wasn't an excuse. I really didn't feel well. I was telling Kelly the truth. He walked me to my car, I climbed in and locked the doors and drove off. I was never so happy to be away from anyone in my life."

"Why?" Carter asked. "He seems like a nice guy. I mean, I guess I only know him from seeing him deliver packages at work."

"Well, I noticed our waitress acting a little funny and like I said, it turns out she has been on a few dates with Kelly." Alana paused, trying to put the words together to tell Carter the remainder of the story.

"Really? Now it's getting interesting." Carter rubbed his hands together and laughed. "Keep going. You can't leave me hanging."

"I guess it's funny now. Friday night not so much." Alana shuddered. "I cornered the waitress and she filled me in. I guess our UPS man has a foot fetish."

"You're joking!" Carter exclaimed. "Kelly?"

"I wish I was, but our waitress sounded pretty convincing. Convincing enough to make me want to leave."

"What did she tell you?" Carter turned around walking backwards as he waited for her to answer. "Come on. Tell me."

"She said he offered to give her a foot massage using the excuse she'd been on her feet all day. Her words were that he *gets off* on women's feet and that's all she was going to say about it." Alana made air quotes with her fingers.

"Wow! I'll never be able to look at him the same again." Carter turned around and shook his head.

"Me either." Alana couldn't help but smile as she watched Carter almost choke from laughing. "I'm so glad I could entertain you this morning."

"I bet." Carter coughed. "Have you talked to him since then?"

"He called the next day. I let it go to voicemail then texted him and told him I still didn't feel well and thanked him for dinner."

"What now?"

"I'll have to worry about that when I see him again. I'll come up with an excuse by then. Maybe I'll tell him John came back. I don't know."

"Tell him you have to go shoe shopping." Carter laughed loudly backing away from her but not far enough.

"You're so funny this morning." Alana tried to reach his arm to pop his arm without luck so she began walking ahead of him.

"Wait up. I'll behave. But seriously, have you thought about going back to the restaurant and talking to the waitress again? See if she'll tell you any more about Kelly." Carter picked up his pace so he could catch up with her.

"The thought has crossed my mind. I'd like to know If what she told me was true or if it was something like a jilted lover thing."

"It would probably be a good idea." Carter agreed.

"I'll have to think about it. I may not want to know much more. After all, I'll still run into him because I'm on his delivery route." She brushed away a piece of hair that had blown in her eyes. "Thanks again for walking with me to get coffee and for letting me talk it through. I wanted to let you know what was going on since you see Kelly now and then. If he asks about me, just tell him you haven't talked to me."

"I needed some coffee so it's no problem. I've got you covered. I'm glad you were smart enough to see what was happening and figure it out." Carter put his hand on her shoulder.

"It's nice to have someone to talk with about this stuff. I might just have to start bringing you along on dates for protection." Alana laughed. "Do you hire out?"

"Go ahead and laugh. I'd be happy to. I wouldn't even charge you. Then I wouldn't have to worry about you."

"You worry about me?" Alana stopped and looked at Carter. She noticed he had shaved which was a little disappointing. She liked his scruffy look.

"Of course, I do. I consider us friends." He stopped next to her, his gaze locking with hers.

"That's really nice to hear." Alana liked the smile on his face. She was glad he was her friend even though they came from different backgrounds. He'd grown up on a farm and was a true cowboy. She was a city girl. She felt comfortable around him, not worrying about anything when she was with him. He was like a big brother. "Sorry, I've been hogging the conversation. How was your weekend?"

"I also had a date and I learned a lot about myself." Carter smirked.

"You did? Who did you go on a date with? A psychic?" Alana laughed.

"Not really. Her name was Angel and she was an expert on horoscopes." He let out a sigh.

"Oh, I bet that was a good time. I seem to remember you don't really believe in horoscopes. Didn't we have that discussion sometime or another? What did she tell you about yourself?"

"I guess I'm an Aries and I'm a selfish lover." Carter brushed his fingernails across his shirt.

"And Angel could tell you that by your zodiac sign?" She snorted.

"That's what she said. She also said we weren't compatible because she's some sign that's a scale or something like that."

"A Libra." Alana explained.

"You know about this crap huh?"

"Not a lot, but enough to be dangerous." Alana raised one eyebrow.

"I guess we were compatible enough for me to buy her dinner, but that was all." Carter held one finger in the air.

"Lucky you," Alana replied. "You would think she would have figured that out before she went on a date with you."

"You'd think. We're both batting a thousand in the dating arena." Carter stopped in place. "We're here. Let's get some coffee and forget about those losers. What do you say?" He opened the door and motioned for Alana to walk through.

"I say life can only get better from here." Alana walked through the door taking her place in line.

She got a strange but pleasurable feeling at the thought of Carter's date being almost as bad as hers. It was comfortable having someone who was experiencing the same thing she was.

Her girlfriends kept telling her there's always another man out there. You have to keep looking. She was tired of looking. All she wanted was to feel safe and understood. Carter was that safe place for now.

"I forgot to tell you; I received a wedding invitation in the mail addressed to John. He must have forgot to fill out a change of address form." Alana smiled.

"Whose wedding?" Carter asked.

"Ron and Pam, I think were the bride and groom names. I don't know who they are. Do you?"

"Really? Yes, I do. I received an invitation also." Carter laughed. "I forgot that John was the one who introduced me to Ron."

"Do you still hang around with him?"

"Sure. He's one of the guys who joins in the pick-up basketball games I play now and then. I run into him a lot at the gym. We've become pretty good friends." Carter explained.

"I thought about being nice and mailing the invitation to Kim, but it was just a fleeting thought." Alana flitted her hand in the air.

"Why don't we go together?" Carter blurted out.

"You're not serious?" Alana turned to face him to make sure he could see just how absurd she thought his suggestion was.

"I'm very serious. John and Kim will probably be there and it'll be fun to see how they react when we show up together."

His expression was serious.

"I don't know, Carter." Alana scrunched up her nose.

"I had planned to go to the wedding. It would be a lot more fun if you go with me. It'll be nice to go and have fun with someone who already knows me. I don't have to worry about trying to impress a date. Promise me you'll think about it." Carter pleaded.

Alana could see the excitement in Carter's brown eyes. He was right, they'd been on so many bad dates lately it would be nice to just go out and have fun with a friend. "I promise I'll think about it."

"That's all I ask," Carter said as he motioned for Alana to give the girl behind the counter her order.

"A café mocha, please."

He placed his order, insisting on paying for both drinks. He wasn't pushy about going to the wedding together but she was beginning to think that it would be a fun night out with a friend.

CHAPTER SIX

"That was a beautiful ceremony." Alana wiped tears from her eyes as she sat back down waiting for the families of the bride and groom to be escorted out of the flower-filled chapel. It was a good thing she always thought to bring a few tissues in her bag. Weddings always made her cry and so did being around so many flowers. "I think they went a little overboard on the flowers though."

"It was very nice." Carter commented as he unbuttoned his jacket and sat back down next to her. "My favorite part of any wedding is the cake."

Laughing, she put her tissue back in her bag. "You don't come to a wedding to listen to the exchange of vows or check out the bridesmaids' dresses?" She shook her head. "You're missing out on the best part."

"No way!" Carter exclaimed. "The cake's the best part. Seeing what combination of cake, frosting, and filling the couple picked is worth sitting through the ceremony."

"You're not serious?" Alana tilted her head and locked her gaze on him.

"Of course, I am." Holding up his fingers, he counted down his list. "The cake's first. Next's whether or not they've got an open or cash bar. After that is the music. Do they hire a band or a DJ? There has to be good music so you can dance. All those things make a wedding."

"Now I know you're not serious. You're just making things up." Alana sat up straight in her chair.

"And you're not?" Carter scoffed. "Who comes to a wedding to check out dresses and vows?"

"I do!" Alana exclaimed. "One of these days I plan to get married and I like to see what's in style, what wedding colors people pick and what kind of ceremony they have. It'll help me when I plan my wedding."

"We're going to have to disagree on what's important." Carter held his hands up in surrender. "When or if I ever get married, everyone's going to be in western wear, there's going to be a huge cake maybe shaped like the state of Texas, all chocolate with raspberry filling and chocolate icing. None of this white icing stuff. Also, no flowers real or not. Maybe tumbleweeds." Carter leaned back in his chair. "Oh, and the bride and groom will ride in on horses."

"Horses? I can't wait to be a guest at your wedding. It sounds like it's going to be very different." Alana laughed.

"Different for you. Not for me. Besides, I thought you're going to be an old cat lady."

"I think I have a few more years before I'm old, then I'll worry about getting the cats. I don't want to start to early and out-live them. Besides I'm having a blast going out on all the fun dates." Alana gave Carter a quick wink and smile as she made air quotes with her fingers.

"You've got this all figured out, don't you?" He leaned over closer. "Don't look now, but here comes John and Kim."

"Where?" Alana looked around to try and see them.

"They must've been sitting at the front of the chapel. They're right behind the last row of family members." Carter turned to look at her instead of down the aisle. "What should we do?"

"I say we pretend not to see them and then if they stop and talk, we act nice and then trash them and what they're wearing when they walk away."

"Be serious for a minute." Carter whispered.

"I'm being serious." Alana grinned. "I really don't care if they see us. I didn't come to the wedding to see them. I came with you as your wedding buddy."

"What the heck's a wedding buddy?" Carter glanced at her with a questioning look on his face.

"A wedding buddy's a friend you can go with to weddings so you don't have to sit at the singles table or worry about being set up with strangers by the bride and groom and you have someone to dance with."

"Do you still get to stay for the reception and have cake?"

Alana patted him lightly on the knee and laughed. "Of course, you do. You can have all the cake you want while I check out the bridesmaids' dresses."

Carter took Alana's hand in his and shook it. "It's nice to meet you wedding buddy."

Alana smiled as she noticed John and Kim walking past them without even noticing. "I think we're in the clear. They just walked by."

Carter turned around to catch their backs as they walked out of the chapel. "I can't believe they didn't see us sitting here."

"Don't worry. I'm sure we'll have an opportunity to run into them at the reception." Alana stood and waited for Carter to stand up and button his jacket. "Besides did you see what Kim was wearing. It was so gaudy."

Snorting, he put his arm around her waist, he led her out into the aisle. "Let's go check out those bridesmaids' dresses and get some of that wedding cake."

****

"Now, that's what I call a wedding cake." Carter took his place in line as they waited to greet the bride and groom. He pointed to the table holding a five-tier wedding cake.

"You're really obsessed with cake, aren't you?" Alana laughed as she got in line beside him.

"Don't look now, but I think we've been spotted." Carter leaned in closer.

"Just act natural. Like we don't even know they're here," Alana replied letting out a laugh.

"What's that about?" Carter asked as he smiled and played along.

"You want them to think we are happy and having a good time. The last thing I want them to think is that we're miserable."

"I'm happy." Carter put his hand on his chest. "I'm having a good time with my wedding buddy and I'm about to have a piece of cake then a few dances. What could be better?"

Rolling her eyes, Alana studied John and Kim. The redhead was slim and willowy, wearing a dress with a lot of cleavage. "Kim looks good."

"You look better."

She nudged his shoulder. "Flatterer."

"I mean it. You look great and I'm glad to be here with you instead of her."

His expressions were becoming easy to read, and she realized he was telling the truth. She shut everything else happening around them out as she looked at him. He was happy. She'd seen him when he was miserable after Kim dumped him and now, looking into his eyes, she saw a changed attitude. "I'm really impressed."

"About what? That I can dance?" Carter asked.

"You." Alana touched his arm lightly. "You've really gotten over Kim."

"I have and I couldn't have done it without you." Carter placed his hand on top of hers. "You've been there for me and helped me out."

"I guess we were lucky we both had each other."
She locked her gaze with his. They were both learning to
be happy.

****

"I'll be right back. Enjoy your cake." Alana pointed
to Carter's second plate of cake he'd returned to their
table with. Laughing, she watched him take a bite, close
his eyes and make some moaning sound. As she made
her way toward the bathroom she was still smiling.
She'd never meet anyone who enjoyed cake as much as
Carter Owens.

Closing the door of the last available stall in the
restroom, Alana could hear the other doors open and
the two women begin to exchange greetings. Listening
closely, she recognized one of the women's voices. It
was Kim.

"It's been a long time since I've seen you. How are
you doing?" the other woman's voice echoed.

"I'm doing great. How about you?" Kim answered.

"I'm good. I noticed you're here with a new date.
What happened to Carter? Was that his name?"

"Oh, you know. I found someone a little more
compatible than Carter. His name is John. Carter was
just so country. I think that's the best way to describe
him."

55

Alana began to fume as Kim's laugh made her skin crawl.

"Country, huh? I always liked Carter. He was so pleasant to be around."

"That was another thing." Kim continued. "He was always so pleasant. It could really be annoying. John's more real. I can be myself around him. When his girlfriend kicked him out like yesterday's trash, I was there to pick up the pieces. It's been good ever since."

"Kicked him out! Yesterday's trash! Carter annoying!" Alana whispered under her breath. Anger began to boil through her body and Kim's laugh was the fuel. Infuriated, she didn't even react to hitting herself with the stall door as she opened it. She stepped out into the lounge area of the restroom and cleared her throat to make sure Kim noticed her. She didn't say anything. She didn't have to. Her eyes were locked with Kim's as she walked towards her.

"Alana," Kim said with hesitation in her voice.

"You're right about John being yesterday's trash and if he makes you happy, I'm glad." Alana moved closer. "But I don't want to ever hear you talk about Carter that way. You treated him horribly. He didn't deserve that from you. He loved you and you hurt him." Alana stepped back when she noticed Kim's expression change from one of surprise to one of fear. "Carter Owens deserves someone so much better than you. Someone who cares about him and accepts him for what and who he is which is a thoughtful, caring man."

Kim didn't say a word. She turned and open the door, disappearing from Alana's view.

Alana sat down in the closest chair trying to calm herself. She didn't want to go back to the table and have Carter ask her any questions. She needed to look as normal as possible and she knew right now her face was probably beet red from anger. There was no way she was going to share with him what happened. He'd already been hurt by Kim. He didn't need to be hurt again. She leaned back in the chair and closed her eyes trying to take a few breaths and slow her heart rate.

"What the hell?" Alana sat back up quickly as she realized she had stood up for Carter to Kim and could have cared less about John.

CHAPTER SEVEN

"You made a wonderful choice in restaurants."
Alana looked around the softly lit restaurant and
adjusted her napkin in her lap. She hadn't been here
before. The atmosphere was very romantic. There were
candles and flowers on each table. Linen napkins and
real silverware.

"I'm glad you approve." Charles smiled. "This is
one of my favorite places to have dinner."

His smile caught her attention. It softened his
face. She had a habit of judging people by their smiles.
Some people forced them, making their face look
unnatural while other people's smile seemed to
accentuate their features. Charles's smile was very nice.

She still couldn't figure out why she agreed to another blind date. She was becoming accepting of her singleness, enjoying her alone time and the quiet space of her apartment. She was taking time to do things she'd always wanted, pottery classes, learning to speak Italian and every now and then, spending time with Carter. Why she would want to try and fit a new relationship in was a huge question she couldn't answer.

Her good friend Tammy convinced her to try again, having only good things to say about Charles. He belonged to her church and she had known him for a number of years. *Tammy better be right about him or she was never going to listen to her again.* So far, he'd been a perfect gentleman and he was very nice looking. He opened the door for her. He pulled her chair out and waited for her to sit down at the table. His manners were a plus on her list.

"Tammy mentioned you're an accountant." Alana broke the silence.

"Yes, I am an accountant," Charles replied.

"What made you decide on that career path?" She wanted to keep the conversation light while learning as much as she could about him.

"My strength was math in school and accounting is an honorable profession."

There was his smile again. It caught her attention every time she saw it. "I agree with that. It's definitely an honorable profession. Was that your first choice for your career or was there something else you wanted to do?"

"Not really."

"I see." Alana waited to see if he would attempt to keep the conversation going by adding on to his comment.

"I did think about becoming a police officer to help people, but it was way too dangerous. I need to have a safe profession with a steady career path."

"Really? It sounds like you gave your future a lot of thought." Alana cocked her head to the side.

"I did. I couldn't put my life at risk on a daily basis." The smile disappeared from his face as his expression became serious. It was as if he entered another world.

"I've always thought policemen were heroes. I mean they deal with danger every day." Alana watched to see if she could bring his smile back.

"I needed a safe profession so I could be around to take care of my mother."

"Your mother? Is she not well? Where's your father? Do you have any brothers or sisters who could help you take care of your mother? I mean so you could do something with your life that you loved." Alana continued asking questions as they popped in her head.

"I had to become an accountant because my father has been gone quite a few years and I have no brothers or sisters. It's only me and Mother." Charles explained.

"I'm sorry about your father but choosing a profession based on how safe it is versus what you want to do isn't a very fulfilling way to live." Alana leaned in toward the table.

"I hardly remember my father."

She felt sorry for him. A little boy losing his father had to be hard.

"How did he die?" Alana asked.

"Oh, he didn't die. He just left. One day I came home from school and mother told me he was gone and wouldn't be coming back." Charles suddenly had a blank stare on his face.

"How awful. And you've never heard from him again?" Alana's heart was breaking. How could someone abandon their child?

"No. Nothing."

"So where does your mother live?" She posed the question reluctantly; almost positive she knew the answer.

"She lives with me. Or I guess I should say I live with her." Charles's smiled returned.

"Oh, I see. How nice for your mother," Alana replied as the thought of strangling Tammy when she saw her again crossed her mind.

"It's nice to have her where I can make sure she's okay. Also, it's nice to be able to come home to the treats she has made me."

"Treats?" Alana squinted her eyes as she asked hesitantly. She knew she wasn't going to like his answer.

"Yes." He nodded enthusiastically. "Every day she makes something different."

Alana could swear the expression of joy on his face made him look like a small child. "That's nice she makes you treats. What about dinner. Do you cook for her then since she has made you treats?" She tried to give him an opportunity to turn back into a grown man.

"No. I don't cook. Mother does all the cooking and cleaning. She doesn't believe in a man having to do any household chores. She takes pretty good care of me." Charles looked down and brushed a piece of lint off his jacket.

"What about your laundry?" Alana couldn't believe she was actually going further into this conversation. She knew his answer wasn't going to make him look any better in her eyes.

"Mother does that also. That's one of the reasons she wants me to meet someone and get married. Someone she approves of, of course." Charles held a finger in the air to make his point. "She wants me to have someone to take care of me if something happens to her."

"I bet." Alana nodded in agreement to keep from suggesting he grow up. "If she does all that for you, I can't imagine how you would be if you were left alone."

"Do you know how to cook and clean?" Charles asked.

"I do, Charles. I would expect anyone I marry to know how to also. I think everyone should be able to take care of themselves." Alana explained.

"You mean all the women you know right?" Charles nodded as he waited for her answer.

Alana couldn't believe what was coming out of his mouth. She was unsure of his age but thought he had to be in his late twenties or early thirties. How could someone his age not know how to do anything for themselves? This had to be one of Tammy's jokes. Alana glanced around the room for Tammy's long, curly red hair. Tammy had to be hiding within eyesight.

"Tammy put you up to this, right?" Alana squinted an eye as she looked at Charles. "She has a great sense of humor. Tell me she convinced you to play a trick on me."

"No, she didn't." He looked offended. "Tammy didn't put me up to anything."

"You're being serious then."

"Why would I not be serious? Everything I'm telling you is the truth. Why would I play a trick on you? I don't know you that well." His expression was solemn.

"All right then." Alana adjusted in her chair. "I think everyone should be self-sufficient. Men too. There's no reason anyone should rely on someone else to take care of their basic needs. Don't you want to know how to cook a meal for someone or do your own laundry, maybe help around the house?" Alana asked. "I'm sure your mother would like a break now and then."

"Why should I want or need to know any of that? I have Mother to take care of me and after I marry, I'll have a wife to take care of me." Charles's voice was strong and forceful.

"And, God forbid, anything should happen to your mother before you find someone to marry, what would you do?" Alana couldn't wait for his answer to this question.

"I'm not sure. I guess I haven't really thought about it." Charles seemed surprised by her question.

Did he really think his mother was going to live forever and take care of him? If he did, he was in for a real surprise. Alana didn't really want to, but there was one more question she needed an answer to.

"When you do get married, is your mother going to be all right with you not living with her?"

"What do you mean?" Charles looked puzzled.

"I just thought you and your new wife would probably want to buy your own house, have your own private space maybe big enough to have room for children. I'm sure you want children." Alana almost cringed as she waited for his reply.

"And big enough for Mother. Or we could just all live with her. I mean, she already has a big enough house and she could teach my wife how to take care of me correctly. Mother could also help with the children. I'm sure whomever I marry will need a lesson or two on how to do things right. Mother is very particular about the way things are done."

"Are you serious, Charles?" Alana asked. "You can't expect a new wife to move in with your mother."

"Why not? Why should we pay for a house when the one my mother owns is perfectly suitable for a family?" Charles answered.

"Maybe your wife's going to want her own home. Some place she can call hers. Maybe do things her way. Is your new wife going to work?" Alana suddenly regretted asking that question.

"Oh no." Charles sat back in his chair, fervently shaking his head back and forth. "Her responsibility will be to take care of me and if we have children, take care of them. I come first, then the kids and then if she has time for anything else, she can have a hobby."

Alana realized he wasn't joking. He was serious about how his life was planned out. The trait of being a mother's boy definitely didn't make her grandmother's list. That was the last straw. Tammy was going to get a serious talk from her when she saw her again, that is if she was still talking to her.

She couldn't bring herself to walk out on another date like she did with Kelly. Maybe she could use this time to talk with Charles and see if she could plant a few seeds that some of the things his mother was telling him were wrong. Maybe the next woman he took out on a date might consider a second.

"Why don't we order?" Alana picked up her menu and tried to find something Charles's mother would approve of.

CHAPTER EIGHT

"I'm feeling a little confused about my date last night. I don't understand why you thought setting me up with Charles was a good idea. I seriously thought you were playing a joke on me, and I was ready to strangle you." Alana leaned back against her couch and covered her face with her hands. "I really don't know how much more of this dating stuff I can take. The old cat lady's looking very good."

"I'm really sorry, but you can't give up that easy," Tammy replied as she took a seat next to Alana on the couch. Friends since college, the two women had seen each other through many bad dates.

"At this point, I don't believe there are any good guys left out there." Alana whispered through her hands.

"You can't be so negative. You have to think positive thoughts. You'll find someone, probably when you are not looking." Tammy insisted.

Alana lifted her head, dropped her hands and glared at Tammy. "I'm trying to stay positive, but then I get set up on dates with men like Charles."

"I know, but he's such a nice guy in a normal setting. Who would've ever guessed he was such a momma's boy?" Tammy shook her head in disbelief. "What a waste of a gorgeous man."

"I'll give you that one. He is nice looking, a sharp-dresser and he smelled really nice, but by looking at him you would never know his umbilical cord was still attached." Alana laughed as she sat up and pulled her feet underneath her on the couch.

"Now you're being just a tad dramatic." Tammy snapped.

"I don't believe so. It wouldn't surprise me at all if Charles never marries and after his mother passes, lives alone the rest of his life trying to figure out how to take care of himself."

"There'll be some desperate woman out there who will marry him." Tammy explained. "After all, I'm sure his mother's going to leave him a lot of money. From what I understand her family was very wealthy."

"Or he'll fall in love with a woman who'll completely change him, try to turn him against his mother or wait until she dies and then spend all her money." A huge smile grew on Alana's face at the thought of all the mischief some woman could cause Charles.

"Don't say that!" Tammy exclaimed.

"Why not?" Alana asked. "You know there's a very good chance it's going to happen."

"No, I don't. Charles isn't that way. He loves his mother and would never do anything to hurt her," Tammy said.

"Let's drop this subject." Alana waved her hands. "Charles is hardly worth wasting our time on. He has enough problems without us adding to them."

"What if we talk about something that has been on my mind for a while now?" Tammy asked.

"Sure. What is it?"

"Why don't you ask Carter out?" Tammy smiled as she waited for Alana's reply.

"What are you talking about. We're just friends!" Alana exclaimed. "We come from completely different backgrounds. But I have to admit, Carter's handsome if you like cowboys."

"Come on. You guys are very cute together plus you have a lot in common. Maybe not how you grew up but both of you were hurt by your exes. I think you'd make a perfect couple." Tammy leaned back against the back of the couch. "Didn't you guys go out together?"

"Just stop right there." Alana held one hand up in the air. "We went to a wedding together as wedding buddies."

"Wedding buddies? What the heck's that?" Tammy asked.

"It's a person you can go to a wedding with so you don't have to sit at the singles table. You can enjoy the ceremony without friends trying to set you up with other single friends," She said with a glare.

"Got it. Wedding buddies huh? I like that idea."

"Besides, I don't want to ruin our friendship. It means too much to me. Carter's my safe place. He's a person I can go to who completely understands what I've already gone through and am currently going through. He's in the same boat."

"Okay. I'll stop." Tammy lifted her hands in surrender

"Thank you." Alana stood up from the couch. "I'm going to get us a glass of wine."

"That sounds good." Tammy stood and followed her into the kitchen, taking a seat at the kitchen island. "By the way, I started going to a female empowerment group. It's very informative and positive. Would you like to join me sometime?"

"Female empowerment? Tell me more about it." Alana poured wine into the two glasses she placed on the island.

"There's a lot of sharing of past experiences where the members have learned and grown. They try to help women learn to be alone and not feel like they need a partner in their lives to make them whole. How to be responsible for your own happiness."

"Why did you start attending a group like that?" Alana asked. "You've always been a strong independent woman."

"I put on a good act, didn't I?" Tammy laughed.

"You mean you felt lonely and unhappy? That surprises me. I mean, you've always been so pulled together and excited about life." Alana took a sip of her wine. This was a side of Tammy she had never seen before. She could see her pale skin blushing as she complimented her.

"I am, but I've always been made to feel there was something missing if I didn't have someone in my life. My family and my friends who are in relationships always ask me when I'm going to find Mr. Right." Tammy ran her fingers through her hair before she continued.

"This group has taught me to realize that everyone who crosses my path adds to my life in one way or another. I don't need to look at every guy I meet as a potential partner or lover, just as a friend or acquaintance. I've been putting too much pressure on myself to find that person who'll complete me. I don't need to be completed. I'm good just the way I am." Tammy twisted her shoulders, showing the pride she had in herself.

"That's interesting. I think that's the way I look at Carter. He's a friend who, right now, I need in my life. You know, I just might go with you sometime." She thought about the list her grandmother had made for her, traits for a life partner. Maybe she was putting too much pressure on herself. Maybe she was trying to put every man she met in a box her grandmother had created for her.

"You may not need everything everyone shares but I think everyone can get something out it." Tammy smiled.

"Let me know the next time you're going and I'll see if I'm free." Alana asked.

"It's a deal."

"You have to promise me one thing though..." Alana paused.

"What's that?" Tammy asked.

"Stop setting me up on blind dates! I'm going to become an empowered woman!" Alana placed her hand on her chest. She liked that idea. "Let's go to dinner. I'm starving."

CHAPTER NINE

"What have you gotten me into, Tammy?"

They sat in folding chairs placed in a circle in the middle of a living room that looked as if it had been decorated in the seventies. The furniture in the room had been pushed back against the walls to make room for the chairs. "I'm getting a strange feeling about this."

After tucking a tote bag under her chair, Tammy reached over and patted Alana's knee. "Don't worry. I remember how I felt the first time I came to one of these meetings. It took me a few of them to feel comfortable enough to talk, but you'll get there."

"Why are we meeting in a house and not a restaurant or meeting room somewhere?" Alana asked as she watched other women join them, taking seats in the circle.

"We take turns meeting at different members' houses. It's a more intimate setting and most of the members feel more comfortable talking than they would if we met somewhere in public." Tammy explained.

The topic for the meeting was written on a whiteboard placed in front of the brick fireplace. *Getting to know yourself more intimately.* If the highlight touched on what first went through her mind, Alana wouldn't even discuss this with her girlfriends much less a room full of strangers. "How in the world did you ever find this group?"

"A woman I work with invited me to come with her to a meeting." Tammy turned and looked at Alana. "I know some of topics we cover can be a little uncomfortable to talk about, but if the only thing you do is listen, you'll learn something from everyone else."

"Uncomfortable?" Alana's voice was a little higher pitched than she intended. "Tammy, I don't even talk to you about this and you're one of my best friends." Alana pointed to the whiteboard in the front of the room.

"That's why I come to these meetings. Subjects covered in here are things our group of friends wouldn't feel right sharing. I thought if you came with me, you would possibly learn somethings and maybe you and I could start talking about these things when we're with all the others. It would be nice to be able to discuss things like this with our friends without being embarrassed or feeling uneasy. Don't you think?"

With a serious expression, Tammy waited for her to acknowledge the suggestion. Alana's rejection to her idea was interrupted by the leader of the group welcoming everyone. She was wearing a long flowing skirt and peasant blouse. Her shoulder-length wavy graying hair along with the dozen bracelets dangling from her arms made Alana think perhaps she'd grown up in the sixties. And wasn't that the era of free love, burn your bra, and all kinds of out of the norm trend-setting ideas?

"Welcome to the weekly meeting of Empowered Women. I see we have a visitor tonight." She pointed at Alana with her long neatly manicured nails. "Why don't you tell us who you are and why you decided to join us tonight."

Alana cleared her throat and adjusted herself in her chair before she spoke. "My name is Alana. I'm here tonight because my friend Tammy invited me to come along with her." Alana pointed to Tammy sitting next to her. "She hasn't told me much about the group except it has helped her become a more empowered woman."

The group applauded along with the leader, her bracelets jingling as she clapped her hands together. "That's wonderful to hear. I'm glad Tammy's sharing information about our group with her friends and is now bringing them along." The leader nodded at Tammy with a smile on her face. "I'm Angela and I'm sure the rest of the group will introduce themselves as we get into the meeting. I hope you all remembered what we're going to cover tonight. You'll notice I've written the topic on the board."

Alana closed her eyes as the leader pointed to the words written in hopefully erasable marker.

"This is a subject you all have been asking to be covered in one of our meetings. Alana, you're in for a big surprise. Feel free to join in or if you don't feel comfortable enough, you can just watch and learn." Angela smiled and then reached behind the whiteboard and took a bag off the closest table. "I asked you to bring a few things with you tonight."

Tammy reached under her chair and took out the tote bag she'd brought with her. A strange feeling ran through her body as Alana wondered what was about to happen. She watched each of the women in the group take a mirror of some kind out of their bags.

"I only had one mirror to bring. We can share if you want." Tammy held up a pink handled mirror like the one Alana's hairstylist used so she could see the back of her hair when she was finished.

The other women were laughing and checking their reflections in their mirrors, straightening their hair or checking their lipstick.

One of the exercises must have to do with learning to appreciate what you saw when you looked in the mirror. That would be a good exercise to empower women. Alana knew most women, including herself, had a negative self-image. Changing the way women think when they see themselves would be a great start to developing empowerment.

Instead of checking her reflection in her mirror, Angela dropped her mirror on the floor in front of her. All the women in the circle including Tammy stood from their chairs and did the same.

"What's happening?" Alana whispered.

"When everyone's ready and feeling comfortable enough, I want you to remove your clothing and stand over your mirror. We're going to get to know ourselves more intimately." Angela reached for the hem of her peasant blouse and began pulling it over her head.

Frozen in her chair, Alana watched in horror as the women around her began to undress. Her worst fear of what would happen tonight was coming true. She couldn't move. She suddenly heard an audible moan which she realized was coming from her.

Each of the naked women stood spread-legged over the mirror they had placed on the floor in front of them. She couldn't look or listen. She wanted to put her hands over her ears so she could block out Angela's instructions on what to look for. Instead, she closed her eyes and prayed this would be over soon.

CHAPTER TEN

"I'm going to be damaged for the rest of my life." Alana placed her head in her hands. "What I saw can't be unseen."

"It wasn't that bad. You're being just a tad dramatic." Tammy laughed as she tossed her tote bag on the kitchen island and took a seat on one of the barstools.

Alana straightened up and glared at Tammy. "You can't be serious! How could you take me to something like that and not warn me what was going to happen? I mean first it was Charles and now I don't know how to even explain what tonight was." Alana opened the refrigerator door, taking out a bottle of wine. She reached for two wineglasses in the cabinet and poured for each of them. "I need a drink."

"You said you wanted to become an empowered woman and part of that involves getting to know yourself more intimately." Tammy reached across the kitchen island and took one of the glasses of wine. "Being an empowered woman means being able to tell your lover what your needs are. Or if you're between lovers, knowing for yourself what your needs are."

"I can't talk to you about this." Alana held her hands up in the air. "This is way out of my comfort zone."

"It's a natural thing. It shouldn't be something you are uncomfortable talking about. One thing I've learned from this group is that women don't take enough responsibility for their own bodies." Tammy straightened up in her chair. "Sure, we go to the doctor every year, spread our legs on the exam table or put our breasts in a vice so we can be told we're healthy. But we don't take the time to get to know how our bodies work and what we can do to make our lives more pleasurable."

"It's not the idea of learning more about my body. I don't mind that, but in a private setting. Maybe read an article or watch a show. It was the idea of doing it in a group of women who I don't know and who don't know me but were willing to strip down completely naked and explore their own bodies in front of me." Alana shook her head. "Maybe I'm not cut out to be an empowered woman if that's one of the requirements."

"We don't strip naked at *all* of our meetings." Tammy laughed. "Maybe you can come back with me to one where we keep our clothes on."

"I don't know, Tammy." Alana scrunched up her nose. "I just don't think I'm ready. I'll never be able to look at those women the same again."

"I didn't think I was ready either, but it's become easier each time I go to be part of the group. I'm very comfortable with all of them and I always come away from the meetings feeling better about myself." Tammy tilted her shoulder and smiled.

"All I can say is good for you. If it makes you feel better about yourself, then you keep going. For me, I'm going to have to think for a while about returning." Alana sipped her wine.

"I'll keep letting you know about the meetings then." Tammy reached across the island and patted her hand. "If you're ready to go back, you're welcome to tag along."

Alana nodded in agreement but deep down she knew it was going to be a long time before she even considered going back. "Please, let's change the subject."

"All right. How's Carter?" Tammy asked. "I haven't heard you talk about him lately."

"He's fine. I haven't seen him in a few weeks. I did talk to him last week. He called just to check in."

"You mean you two haven't seen each other for that long? You haven't been to anymore weddings as wedding buddies? That's pretty unusual for you guys, isn't it?" Tammy asked.

"It is, come to think of it." Alana wondered what Carter had been doing. They'd been frequently talking, having lunch or connecting somehow. He was definitely not the person she wanted to vent to about the meeting Tammy had dragged her to but she would like to catch up and make sure he was doing all right.

"You should call him. I'm sure he wouldn't mind if you did," Tammy said.

"I know he wouldn't mind. I just don't want to bother him." Alana waved her hand in the air. "Who knows, maybe he's found someone else to spend time with. He did say he wanted to tell me about a few dates he'd gone on. Maybe one of those dates worked out for him."

Alana placed her hand on her stomach as it began to twist into knots. She realized she and Carter had become closer since they had something in common. She started to depend on him to be there and listen to all her crazy date stories, but she hadn't had any of those lately besides Charles. She could always call him and tell him about Charles. Or maybe he'd found someone else and he didn't need her anymore. Some of the feelings she had when John dumped her suddenly came flooding back.

CHAPTER ELEVEN

"This is really nice." Alana took a seat in the chair Marcus had pulled out for her. She'd felt a little underdressed when she saw him wearing an expensive suit and tie. She was wearing a simple black A-line dress with only a few accessories and a pair of stilettos.

She took a minute to glance around the dining room to take in the beautiful decor. Romano's had pulled out all the stops with decorations. She'd been wanting to have dinner here since they opened. They were already in the car when Marcus told her where they were going. She felt guilty because she had promised Carter they could come here together one night. She had even put their names down on the restaurant waiting list for next month. She would have to let him know about tonight. She wanted him to hear it from her.

"I've never been here before. I heard there was a long wait for reservations," Alana said.

"Not if you know the right person." Marcus winked at her as he took a seat across the table. "A friend of a friend works here. He managed to fit us in."

"You'll have to tell him thank you from me. I've been wanting to have dinner here since it opened." Alana couldn't stop admiring the objects adorning the shelves on the walls. "I heard all the decorations are from Italy. One of the lawyers at work told me what the owners spent on decorations would buy someone a nice home."

"That's probably true." Marcus nodded as he adjusted his jacket and tie. "I don't know the owners yet, but I plan on knowing them before too long. It couldn't hurt to have a few more influential people in my life."

Alana turned her gaze to see the look in Marcus's eyes. When they'd met, he'd made it obvious he liked knowing people of wealth and influence and liked dropping their names. What he saw in her was a mystery. She wasn't wealthy. Marcus knew her family didn't come from a line of well-known people. They were common Midwesterners. She always thought Marcus would find a wealthy socialite.

After giving their drink orders to their waiter, Alana looked around the room. She was sure there wouldn't be anyone she knew dining here. It was much too expensive for anyone she was acquainted with. Every now and then Marcus would wave and say hello to someone he recognized.

She was getting the impression he brought her here for the purpose of being seen dining at a high-end restaurant by people of wealth. He made sure to tell her they were going someplace special but not where. They *were* somewhere special. Special for him not for them. It wouldn't have mattered who he brought with him, as long as he wasn't alone. He was here to see and be seen.

Deciding to make a trip to the ladies' room as Marcus continued to make his presence known to the other diners, Alana took her napkin from her lap and began to stand. She caught a glimpse of Carter with a date being seated at a table across the dining room.

Marcus was too busy chatting with whoever he recognized, he didn't even notice she was going to leave the table. Dropping back down in her seat, she placed her napkin back in her lap just as the waiter brought their drinks.

She waited patiently for Marcus to make a production of tasting the wine the waiter had poured in his glass. He twirled the wine in the bottom of the glass then held it to his nose.

"Is this one of your most expensive wines?" Marcus twirled the wine in the glass again and took another sniff.

To her wine was wine. As long as it wasn't too sweet or sour, she was good with it. It could come in a cardboard box or a twist top bottle. As long as she liked the flavor, it was good. She learned when she was younger, while attending a wedding shower for a friend, not to drink a lot of wine in one sitting. It gave her the worst hangover, barely able to open her eyes the next morning.

Marcus finally gave his approval of the wine and the waiter filled her wineglass. Not waiting for the waiter to fill Marcus's wine- glass, Alana picked up her wine and took a drink. She had waited long enough and she needed this. She also wanted the waiter to leave because he was blocking her view of Carter and his date.

She and Carter had discussed coming here together sometime so they could find out what the hype was about. They both loved Italian food and had heard the food here was as close to authentic as you could get. They'd promised each other they wouldn't come here with anyone else until they could come together. She couldn't believe he broke their promise and brought someone else here first. Of course, she didn't want him to see her here either or he would know she did the same.

"Timothy." Marcus held his arm straight up in the air as he yelled across the restaurant.

Alana held her breath and tried no to look in the direction of whoever Marcus was greeting. She knew if she did, Carter would see her. Everyone in the restaurant stopped and looked in Marcus's direction which meant they probably saw her. How could they not. She sank down a little in her chair waiting until things calmed down before she glanced in Carter's direction.

"That's my financial planner. I should introduce you to him. He could give you some great advice on how to invest your money. I'm sure he would give you a discount since you know me." Marcus had a smug smile on his face as he took a drink of his wine.

"You certainly know a lot of people here tonight." Alana made an attempt to change the subject.

Marcus placed his elbows on the table and leaned in and winked at her, oozing confidence with his hundred-dollar haircut, perfectly groomed eyebrows and goatee. "You have to hang out with the right crowd if you're going anywhere in life."

Alana could tell he was very serious which made her wonder if he ever just had fun. Instead of going out to dinner to enjoy the company of your date and a nice meal, Marcus made it a business opportunity. "The people you hang out with don't have to reflect what you want to do with your life. You should enjoy their company."

"That's true. If you want to trudge along in life with not much to show for your hard work, then you hang out with people that feel and do the same. I want to make something out of myself. I'd like to own my own successful business someday. I'd like to retire wealthy. I plan to work hard enough to make that a reality. Knowing people in that position will help me make that happen." Marcus took another drink of his wine as he glanced directly at her.

"What if you want to enjoy your life as you go instead of waiting until you retire to enjoy yourself? What if you work hard and have fun now instead of later?" Alana kept her gaze locked with his. "I enjoy spending time with my friends, talking, getting to know what they like, experiencing new adventures with them. To me that's what I call a success."

"I brought you here tonight. We can look at this from both your point of view and mine. You're here because you're having dinner with me and enjoying my company, and I'm here to hang out with influential people and to also have dinner with you." Marcus lifted his glass as if he was making a toast.

Alana faked a smile and toasted him. She realized she was definitely in second place when it came to his priorities but he was supposed to be *her* first priority. He reminded her of the boy in kindergarten who didn't share his candy. She leaned back in her chair trying to decide exactly how she should handle the situation. Should she stay and risk the chance of Carter seeing her? It didn't matter. Across the dining room, he waved at her from his table.

CHAPTER TWELVE

Alana's ringing cell phone woke her from a dream of Carter running away from her. No matter how fast she ran, she couldn't catch him. She was breathing hard and getting nowhere. He kept running farther away.

Taking time to adjust her eyes and calm her breathing, she saw it was Carter calling. She'd spent the night thinking how to explain why she was at the restaurant. Not with him, but with another person. She hadn't known Marcus would be taking her there. She'd broken her promise to Carter, but *he'd* broken his promise to her.

"Good morning." Alana adjusted her pillows as she sat up in bed.

"Good morning. How are you doing?"

She held the phone away from her ear because Carter's voice was too cheery and upbeat for this early in the morning. She hadn't even had her coffee. "I'm good. What about you?"

Not wanting to spend time skirting around the issue, she brought up the restaurant. "How did you like Romano's last night?"

"That's why I'm calling." Carter answered. "I wanted to explain to you why I was there last night."

"You don't have to explain to me." Alana interrupted. "Really it's fine."

"I feel like I do because you and I planned to go there together." Carter paused; his voice filled with apology.

She didn't say anything, letting the silence in the air linger. They could go back and forth all morning about feeling bad.

"My boss's niece, Charlotte, is visiting. He asked me to show her around. She's shadowing me at work. He asked me to take her to dinner because he and his wife already had plans and he didn't want her being bored while they were gone."

"I see." Alana adjusted her position as she listened.

"Anyway, he suggested Romano's. I guess they have a standing reservation there on Friday nights and he didn't want to take the chance they would lose their table." Carter became silent.

"That was nice of you to spend the evening with her. Charlotte, right? I hope you guys enjoyed Romano's." Alana continued. "I was going to call you and tell you Marcus surprised me and took me to dinner there."

"What did you think?" Carter asked.

"It was really good. Expensive, but really good. I would go back to celebrate something. I couldn't afford to just go there for dinner." Alana laughed.

"I agree. It was a good thing my boss picked up the bill."

"How long is Charlotte here? Maybe you can take her there again." Alana asked.

"She leaves tomorrow. Thank God." Carter whispered the last of his remark.

"What?" She wanted to make sure she'd heard correctly.

"I said thank God." He laughed.

"Why do you say that? She looked like a nice person." Alana sat forward waiting for his explanation.

"Not only did she eat her meal, but she finished mine too and dessert on top of that." Carter chuckled. "Oh, and she's a thief."

"Really?" Alana laughed wondering if she heard him correctly. "A thief? Did she steal something from the restaurant?"

"Yes. The salt and pepper shakers and her napkin. What in the world would you do with a used napkin?" His voice expressed his frustration. "She also stole from me."

"She stole from you? What did she take from you?" Alana was really interested in their conversation now.

"I always keep a pack of gum, a few cigars in case I'm on a long trip and get bored, and also some money in the console of my car." He stopped for a second. "After I took her home, I opened my console to get a piece of gum and it was empty. Besides me, she was the only person in my car and I know I just put a pack of gum in before I picked her up."

"What the hell!" Alana exclaimed. "You think she's going to smoke the cigars?"

"I don't know, but I paid good money for those." Carter grumbled.

"I'm sure you did. I would probably have gone for the cigars also. I love the smell of a good cigar." Alana took a deep breath imagining how one would smell.

"My point is she's a thief," Carter said. "I'm not sure what to do. I mean I probably had fifty dollars in the console plus my cigars. I could care less about the gum."

"You said she's leaving town so my suggestion is to not mention it. If your boss asks how dinner went, lie." She laughed. "And don't volunteer to take her out to dinner again if she comes back to town."

"I don't plan on saying anything to my boss and I definitely won't be volunteering again. I'll come up with some kind of excuse. I'd like to ask her what she was thinking though." Carter paused. "By the way, how was your date with Marcus?"

"Not quite as exciting as yours," Alana replied.

"Are you going to see him again?"

"No!" She exclaimed.

"That was a quick answer. Almost as quick as my answer about Charlotte." Carter chuckled.

"He was there to be seen by all the wealthy people who dine there. He wasn't there because he wanted to take me to a nice place and spend an enjoyable evening. He wanted to be seen, heard, and let it be known he felt like he belonged in their crowd. It was embarrassing to tell the truth." Alana explained, cringing at the memory of Marcus drawing attention to himself.

"I've always thought he was a jerk. I remember when I first met him he asked me about my family. Where they're from and what they did for a living. He was sizing me up to see if I was worth his time. I guess it was a no because he doesn't have much to say to me anymore," Carter said.

"Why did you introduce him to me then?" Alana asked.

"He just happened to be around. You were still with John then. I didn't know you two would eventually go out on a date." Carter laughed. "Besides I don't think I should be deciding for you who you go out with."

"I thought we're friends, Carter," Alana said. "I would be the first to tell you if I knew anything bad about someone you planned to go out with. That's what friends are for. If I knew Charlotte, I would definitely have told you to run far away." She slashed her hand through the air vehemently.

Alana suddenly remembered what she was dreaming before Carter called her. Her heart began to beat faster as she saw him running away from her as she chased after him. Was her dream trying to tell her something? What was it? She began to feel ill.

"I've got to go, Carter. I'll call you later."

Ending the call, she placed her head in her hands, breathing deeply to keep from throwing up. She lay back against her pillow, a deep sadness washing through her body.

CHAPTER THIRTEEN

"Are you ready?" Alana asked as she took a seat on her couch next to Carter. "I've done a lot of research."

"I can't believe I let you talk me into this," he said hesitantly.

"Please, don't back out now. We talked about this and decided we would give it a try together. You and I've gotten through this past year and it's time we both find happiness again."

She watched his expression to see if she could tell what he was thinking. He leaned back against the couch and sighed as he poured a few pieces of candy from the package on the coffee table into his mouth.

"What do we say? What kind of car I drive, how much money I make? Can I mention that I play the guitar?" Carter mumbled as he chewed the candy.

"I didn't know you played the guitar." Alana was surprised by his remark.

He shrugged. "I do but Kim hated it. She always told me I needed to take more lessons."

"Seriously? What does she know? You'll have to play for me sometime. We'll definitely put down you play the guitar. Let's get started then." Alana clapped her hands together then held one out for Carter to share his candy as she reached for the tablet lying on the coffee table.

Carter poured the last few pieces of candy out in her hand then wadded up the paper package and placed it on the table.

"I don't want to take your last pieces." Alana looked at the lonely few pieces of chocolate in her hand.

"Take them. I've had enough."

Alana looked at Carter's smile and for some reason she remembered the boy in kindergarten who didn't share his candy with her. Popping the pieces of candy in her mouth, she opened her tablet.

"I read so many reviews of each of these sites and I think the best one for you to start with is this one. It's full of women looking for a cowboy." Smirking, she pointed at the list she'd made.

"I can't believe I let you talk me into signing up on a dating site." Carter scrunched up his nose.

"Look, you and I've tried dating for ourselves and you have to admit, we haven't had the best of luck." Alana laughed.

"You're right about that. We could write a book." He smiled. "What's the first thing we have to do?"

"We need to fill out a form with information about you, your likes and dislikes and what you desire in a mate. I thought if we did it together, we could help each other out with the about us part." Alana pointed to the form she had pulled up on her tablet.

"I know it's hard for me to talk about myself. I like to think I have wonderful qualities, but I know I'm not quite perfect." Alana placed the back of her hand on her forehead as she leaned back against the arm of her couch.

"You always make me laugh." Carter patted her knee. "That's one of the qualities you need to put down on your form."

Alana managed a smile as she let what Carter just said sink in. She made him laugh. "I can say the same about you. We always manage to laugh a lot when we spend time together."

"We can list that as a positive for both of us. We both have a sense of humor." He glanced down at the tablet to read what else they needed to figure out.

She couldn't seem to break her gaze or get past Carter's comment.

"What else?" He asked as he locked eyes with Alana. "Are you all right?"

"Yes. Yes. I'm fine." She took a breath and began to read off the first question on the form.

"What's the top trait you're looking for when considering whether to date someone?" She watched closely while he thought about his answer.

"For me it's going to have to be trust. I mean after all we went through with John and Kim; I don't think I want to go through something like that again." Carter rubbed the back of his neck.

"You're right about that. Trust is very important. It really hurt when John broke that trust."

"I really trusted Kim also. I think that's what bothered me the most. There's one plus though." Carter paused.

"Plus? What would that be?" Alana couldn't wait to hear the upside from someone betraying your trust.

"Whoever we find or date in the future, they'll have someone they can trust 'til the end of time."

Alana's heart skipped a beat.

"We both know how much it hurts to have someone let you down like they did."

She could see Carter was extremely proud of finding a positive from their past relationships.

"You're right." Alana locked eyes with Carter again as she listened to him talk. She could trust him. He made her laugh; he shared his candy and she knew she could trust him 'til the end.

"I know I'm right. We'll make our future relationships work." Carter smiled, looking directly at her. "What's the next question?"

"Is support from the person you're in a relationship with a top priority?" Alana pretended she was reading the questions from the form but instead they were coming from her heart.

"Of course. Next to trust, having the support of the people in your life is very important. So yes, it's a top priority." Carter smiled.

She took a breath as she tried to manage asking the next question that was on her mind. "What about showing kindness toward you and others? I think that's a good quality to have."

"I'd say that's important also. I know Kim could be a real bitch at times. I can remember being embarrassed a few times when she was upset about something. Everyone within ear shot knew it also." He shook his head.

Alana could tell Kim had dominated their relationship. Carter must have really cared about her to put up with some of her actions for as long as he did. He had been hurt. She could see it in his eyes when he talked about his past relationship.

"I'm really sorry you went through all that with Kim."

"Thanks, Alana. You've been a good friend this past year. In fact, I would say you're the best friend I have."

It was all she could do to keep from crying. Speaking was out of the question, so she smiled. Was Carter Owens the person she'd been praying for? He had every one of the qualities on her grandmother's list. He was the answer to her prayer.

CHAPTER FOURTEEN

"Thanks for helping me with my profile. I've already had two people contact me. You must have made me sound more exciting than I really am." Carter laughed.

"That's wonderful but don't sell yourself short." Alana placed her elbow on her desk and leaned her cheek into her hand while balancing her cell phone. She tried to keep regret out of her voice. "What did you think about them?"

"I haven't had a chance to check their profiles yet. I plan to do that tonight after work. I've been really busy today or I would've done it on my break."

"You'll have to let me know what you think." Alana made another attempt to show him she was excited for him. She was afraid if she told him what she was really thinking he would never want to share with her again.

"What about you? Have you had anyone contact you?" Carter asked.

"No." Alana quickly lied. She knew she couldn't tell him she hadn't submitted her profile yet. She wanted to tell him the truth, that she didn't want to put her profile up on the dating site. She didn't want to be matched up with anyone but him.

"You put your profile up when you put mine up, didn't you?" Carter asked.

"Of course." Alana squinted her eyes. She hated lying to him but she just couldn't tell him the truth. Not yet.

"I'm sure you'll have some contacts soon." His voice softened.

"I'm sure. I'm really in no hurry. You'll have to call or text me tonight when you've gone through the profiles and let me know what you think and if you're going to ask them out." Alana could only imagine how hard it was going to be for her to listen to him talk about other women. Especially ones he was considering dating. She wasn't sure she was ready for that. "I have to get back to work. I'll talk to you later."

She ended the call and laid her head down on her desk. She needed to figure out how she was going to handle her feelings for Carter before he found someone else.

****

Tucking her legs underneath her, Alana pulled a blanket from the back of her couch and wrapped it around herself. She found the dating site on her tablet and refreshed her memory on how to upload her profile.

She took a deep breath as she debated hitting the submit button. "I either do this or tell him how I feel." Her decision was made for her when she received a text from Carter.

I've read through the profiles of the women who contacted me and I don't think I'll be getting in touch with either one of them.

"Thank you." Alana whispered as she closed her eyes and looked upward. Now she had to decide how to answer him.

I'm sorry they didn't work out. I'm sure you'll get another chance.

Alana put her legs on the floor and leaned forward with her phone in her hand waiting for his reply.

Maybe this dating site thing isn't right for me. Maybe I should just leave it up to fate to find the right person for me.

Don't give up so quickly, Carter. I'm sure someone will contact you who you'll find interesting.

I hope so. I'll keep you updated. Nite.

"If Carter and I are meant to be, maybe this is the way to find out."

Alana looked over her profile one more time to make sure it was just like she wanted and then pressed submit. It was out of her hands now. Carter said maybe he should leave his dating life in the hands of fate. She hoped she had given fate a small nudge in the right direction.

****

Alana woke to her alarm. She kept her eyes closed as she reached toward her nightstand and felt around until she found her cell phone. Pushing the snooze button, she rolled over attempting to get a few more minutes of sleep before she had to face the day. The attempt was pointless. Her mind began to race with thoughts of what she had to accomplish at work, what she needed to take care of around her apartment, and of course, Carter. She couldn't help but feel she was hiding something from him.

"I give up." Alana sat up and threw her legs over the edge of her bed. Removing her nightgown and tossing it on the bed, she took clean underwear from the top drawer of her dresser and stepped into the bathroom to turn the water on in the shower.

She wanted to check the dating site to see if anyone tried to contact her. She wanted to know but then she didn't want to know. Carter was the only person she was interested in hearing from.

Why she had the same sinking feelings now she had when John dumped her for Kim she didn't know. She and Carter weren't in a relationship. They were friends and nothing more. She didn't want to lose him as a friend because of her actions. She was trying to help him regain his confidence and get past the hurt Kim had inflicted on him. He was doing the same for her.

If that was all it was, why was he so prominent in her thoughts? Why did she think about him first thing when she woke in the morning and last thing when she fell asleep at night? If they were just friends, why did it hurt to think of him finding another woman to spend time with besides her? If they were just friends, why was she crying?

Alana put her face under the water to make the tears falling from her eyes disappear into the stream.

CHAPTER FIFTEEN

Tapping her toes on the floor under the table, Alana waited for Carter to show. He had picked the closest restaurant for both of them to meet. She wasn't a big fan of Chinese but she wanted to see him so she was willing to meet him wherever. He'd been so busy lately with work but he'd let her know several women had contacted him on the dating website and he was looking at their profiles. He hadn't had a lot of time for her. She finally spotted him walk through the front door.

"I'm so sorry." A breathless Carter sat down on the chair across from her. "I got out of work later than I planned. I had problems with my noon broadcast and the day just went downhill from there. I should have called you."

"It's all right. I haven't been here that long." Alana lied. It seemed she'd been doing that a lot lately when it came to Carter.

"Have you ordered?"

"No. I was waiting for you and trying to decide what I wanted." She smiled.

"That's right. I forgot. You don't really like Chinese." Carter squinted his eyes. "Sorry."

"It's fine. I'm trying to develop new tastes. It not my favorite, but I do like some things."

"Next time you get to choose." He laughed.

"It's a deal." Picking up the menu, she pretended to look through it even though she had decided twenty minutes ago what she wanted. "Tell me how your dates have been going?"

"I've only been out on one new date," Carter said as he glanced through his menu.

"I thought you'd been contacted by several new people."

"I was, but I only thought one of the women sounded interesting. We met up a few days ago." He didn't look up.

"How did it go?" She tried to play it cool, pretending she was reading her menu.

"We had a nice conversation. She was interesting and we did have a few things in common. She liked sports and was an avid reader."

"That's good. Isn't it?"

Carter looked at her. "Have you ever been talking to someone and they don't look you directly in the eyes?"

"I don't think so." Alana was confused by his question. "Why?"

"That's what she did all night. It was like she was always looking for someone or something else instead of talking to me." Carter paused. "It was really strange."

"It must have really bothered you."

"Here, let me show you what I mean." He began looking off in the corner of the room as he continued. "The weather has been beautiful lately. What's the latest book you've read and did you like it?"

She snorted. "I see what you mean. That would drive me crazy."

"I know. I kept trying to get her to look at me and she would for a few seconds then she would return to staring at the wall or whatever." Carter shook his head. "What about you? Have you had anyone contact you?"

"I've had a couple of contacts, but like you I didn't find them interesting enough to answer. I'm not really sure I like this dating website stuff." Alana scrunched up her nose.

"I guess I figure it's not hurting anything to leave my profile out there. Maybe one of these days the right person will contact me. You never know." He motioned for the waitress.

"You never know." Interlocking her fingers in front of her as she watched Carter give the waitress his order, she wondered if he would find someone else before she had the courage to tell him how she felt.

****

"I do have something I want to ask you." Carter pushed his empty plate forward, placing his elbows on the table and looking at Alana.

"Sure. What is it?"

"I got a wedding invitation in the mail yesterday from my old college roommate. I'm supposed to be his best man." Toying with his chopsticks, he glanced up at her. "We had so much fun at Ron and Pam's wedding, I thought I would see if you wanted to be my wedding buddy again."

"We did have a good time." Alana smiled as she remembered how much cake Carter had manage to eat. "I'd love to. When's the wedding?"

"Next month, but before you put it on your calendar, I need to tell you all the details."

She sat back in her chair and placed her hands in her lap. "All right. Fill in the details."

"The wedding's in Italy." Carter paused.

"Italy? You're joking right?" Alana watched and waited for Carter to tell her he was just kidding.

"I'm not joking." Carter shook his head. "Trey's one of my best friends. We met the first day of college as we moved into our dorm room. We did everything together in college. We stayed roommates when we moved in to our frat house. He went home with me once or twice for holidays. I taught him how to ride a horse and we did some chores around the farm. We promised to be each other's best man. I would really like to go to the wedding."

"Of course. I think you should go. After all, you promised him, but you don't have to ask me to go along with you. I mean Italy. What a chance for you to have a great trip." Alana explained.

"I don't want to go alone. You see, all our other friends who'll be going are married or have a significant other. It's going to be a small group. I would be a third wheel. Also, I'm not a good traveler if I travel alone. I thought if you went with me, we could do some sightseeing, eat some real Italian food which would probably put Romano's to shame."

"You're serious." Alana watched his expression to see if she could read his thoughts.

"Yes, I am." Carter nodded.

"I've always wanted to go to Italy and it would be a once in a lifetime chance." She paused, looking past him, thinking about it. "I really don't know if it's a good idea though, Carter." She squinted her nose and shook her head.

"Why not?" Carter leaned forward. "We make great wedding buddies. We both could use a vacation away from here. We both need to have some fun instead of worrying about work and dates and all the stuff that goes along with them. Besides, all we're going to be out is our flights and sightseeing costs. Everything else is paid for. Just think of all the cake and dancing. You can check out the bridesmaids' dresses. What do you say?"

"Really? Everything?"

"If I read the invitation right, it said they've rented out a villa that's been converted into a boutique hotel and there's enough room for everyone in the wedding party. The pictures look amazing. I'll have to send them to you."

"I have to admit, it would be fun." She bit her lip as she considered the invitation. She'd always wanted to travel. John had no interest in seeing other countries. The only trip they'd been on was to Las Vegas and she'd paid for everything.

"There'll be wine, pasta, pizza, lasagna, salad, and I'm sure plenty of Italian desserts. Just imagine all the food." Carter rubbed his hands together as he listed off her favorite things.

"I'm in. You just convinced me." She sat up straight in her chair. "There's nothing like Italian food to get me to say yes."

"Great. I'll RSVP as soon as I get home. We're going to have a great time. I just know it." Carter held up his glass of water for a toast.

Alana picked up her glass and tapped it against his. "I can't wait. Thank you so much for including me. We're going to Italy."

CHAPTER SIXTEEN

"It's beautiful here." Alana twirled around on the stone patio of the Italian villa on the Amalfi coast then stopped and pointed toward the edge of the patio. "Look, you can see the water from here and the houses of all the people in the villages stacked on the side of the mountain. I can't imagine how wonderful it would be to live here."

It was no surprise that Carter was an easy person to travel with. Seated side by side on her couch they'd made the flight arrangements and discussed what they wanted to see when they got there. He'd even carried her luggage for her, teasing just a bit about weight of her suitcase, how it must be filled with stilettos.

"I have to agree with you. I've never been anywhere so beautiful." Carter smiled as he watched her. "I'm really glad you came with me."

"That's the Tyrrhenian Sea." A male voice made Alana turn. "I'm glad you both could make it."

She watched as Carter walked toward him, grasp his hand with one of his, and wrap the other around him. He looked the same age and height as Carter with blonde hair and a nice tan.

"Trey. It's good to see you man."

"You too, Carter. How long has it been? Two years?" Trey asked.

"I'm not sure. All I know is it's been too long." Carter motioned toward her. "I want you to meet a good friend of mine. Alana Andrews. Alana, this is Trey Scott, the groom."

"It's a pleasure to meet you, Alana." Trey stepped forward and took her hand. "I can see you're enjoying the view as much as we do."

"It's absolutely beautiful." Alana turned to glance at the water again.

"Why did you guys decide to get married in Italy?" Carter asked.

"Cynthia has always wanted to visit Italy so when we got engaged, we decided to combine the two, a trip to Italy and our wedding." Trey's expression showed his approval of their decision.

"I'm glad you did. It gives me a reason to visit also." Carter smiled.

"I can't wait for you to meet Cynthia. She's off somewhere with the women of the wedding party." Trey patted Carter's shoulder. "If you guys had gotten here just a few hours earlier, you could have joined them, Alana."

"We'll meet her when they return. For now, I think I should go unpack and get settled. It was a long flight." Alana reached for the luggage she had left by one of the patio tables.

"I can show you guys to your room." Trey turned around to head into the villa.

"Room?" Alana mouthed to Carter. Shrugging, he reached for his suitcase. She followed Trey and Carter as they made their way down a long hallway of stone walls and windows then up a flight of stairs.

"This is it." Trey reached for the knob and opened the door. "The rooms are really nice. The room key is on the table. I'm sure you guys will find everything you need. If not, you can let the front desk know and they can find it for you or tell you where you can find it."

"Carter and I are sharing a room?" Alana moved her hand back and forth between her and Carter while she waited for Trey to reply.

"I thought you two were..." Trey paused. "A couple. I mean I sent the invitation to you and your significant other."

"I guess I should've made sure. That was on me. Kim and I broke up almost a year ago. Alana and I are just really good friends." Carter attempted to explain.

"I'm sorry, but there aren't any more rooms. There are just enough for the wedding party and guests." Trey shook his head in apology.

Alana looked at Carter noticing the concerned expression on his face. "Don't worry, Trey. We'll make it work. I'm sure everything will be fine."

"Are you sure?" Trey asked.

Exchanging glances with Carter, she nodded.

"Of course, it'll be just fine." Carter assured him.

"If you're sure." Trey looked at both of them.

"I can't wait to see what the rooms look like. If they're anything like the view outside, I'm sure they'll be amazing." Alana smiled attempting to calm the tension.

She rolled her suitcase through the door and left it at the end of the bed as she walked toward the double patio doors in awe of the view. The doors were lined with navy blue curtains that matched the headboard on the bed and the bed scarf carefully placed at the end.

"You can see everything from here. Come check out this view, Carter. We even have our own patio." Waving her hand to beckon him forward, she kept looking out the doors.

"I'll let you two get settled. We're planning to have drinks on the patio in a few hours. Hopefully, you guys will join us." Trey waved as he walked out of view.

Carter placed his suitcase at the end of bed beside hers and joined her at the window. "Are you sure you're all right with us sharing a room? I can find somewhere else to stay. Maybe I can sleep on the patio."

"It'll be fine." Alana turned around to face the room. "Everything will be fine. I mean, what could be better? We're in Italy at one of the most beautiful villas with this view." She turned and pointed out the patio doors.

"I tell you what." Carter smiled.

"What?" Alana asked.

"I'll let you choose your side of the bed."

"Deal." Alana smiled as she ran toward the side of the bed closest to the window and fell back into it. "I'll take this one."

****

Getting ready in their room hadn't been awkward at all. He'd showered first while she relaxed on the patio, then she took her time getting dressed in the bathroom.

"How's the room working out?" Trey asked as they walked out onto the downstairs patio.

"It's beautiful." Alana smiled as she pulled a lace wrap around her bare shoulders. She was sure being by the water it could be a little cool in the evening. Her sundress wouldn't be enough to keep her warm.

"I hope it will work." Trey whispered as he moved closer to them. "I'm really sorry about the mix up."

"Don't worry." Carter smiled and winked at Alana. "We worked it out. We'll be fine."

"I'm glad to hear that. I want you guys to meet Cynthia." Trey motioned for them to follow him. "Cynthia, this is Alana Andrews and my old college roommate, Carter Owens."

"It's a pleasure to meet you, Alana. I've heard so much about you, Carter, I feel like I already know you. Trey talks about your adventures all the time." Cynthia shook both their hands.

Alana could see the love between Cynthia and Trey as they glanced at each other and smiled. Both of them blond-haired but Cynthia was a little fairer skinned than Trey with green eyes instead of blue. They were going to have beautiful children. This had to be the most wonderful feeling, starting their life together with a wedding in Italy.

"You two help yourselves to something to drink. Tonight's for relaxing and enjoying everyone's company because tomorrow's going to be a busy day." Cynthia pointed toward the bar on the side of the patio. "I don't know if Trey told you but we have the rooms booked through the weekend so you don't have to leave until then if you want to stay a few extra days and sightsee while you're here."

"He did. We planned on staying a few days after the wedding. Both Alana and I are big fans of Italian food. We're going to check out some of the restaurants." Carter looked at Alana for her approval.

"I'm so glad. That sounds like fun." Cynthia smiled as she pointed toward the doorway. "Excuse me, but I see some friends I need to greet. It was nice to meet both of you."

Alana watched as she disappeared into the crowd then reappeared motioning for Trey.

"I guess I need to join her. You guys get a drink and enjoy yourselves." Trey disappeared as fast as Cynthia.

"It looks like we're on our own. I see food over there. I don't know about you but I'm starving." Carter pointed in the direction of the bar.

"Me too. Let's go." Alana took Carter's hand and led him toward the bar. The heels of her stilettos and his cowboy boots clicking against the stone of the patio.

There were salami and fig crostinis, potato and mozzarella croquets, fresh mozzarella and sun-dried tomatoes, olives of every kind, and wine. So much food and wine they would have no problem finding enough to eat or drink.

They both filled plates with a variety of available food and each took a glass of wine then found a small empty table.

"I can't believe we're in Italy. It's even more beautiful than I imagined." Alana took a sip of her wine.

"I'm glad we decided to do this. I'm already more relaxed and enjoying myself." Carter leaned back in his chair.

"I am too. Thanks for asking me to join you. We're going to have a good time while we're here." All she wanted was for both of them to have a nice time and enjoy being away from all the pressure of work and relationships.

CHAPTER SEVENTEEN

"Are you having fun?" Carter pulled out a chair at their table for Alana to sit down.

"I am." She glanced at the crowd of people they had just been with, all dancing and laughing. The men's jackets hung on the back of their chairs; the women's shoes scattered around the tables. "I'm dancing on the patio of a villa in Italy. I have a view of the sea. There's enough food and wine for the entire city. How could I not be having a good time?" Alana put her arms in the air and twirled around in a circle before she flopped down in a chair. "What about you?"

"I'm having a great time. I really needed this." Carter took the last drink of his wine. "Getting away was a great idea. I'm going to get us another glass of wine. I'll be right back." He stood and walked toward the bar.

Alana leaned her head in her hand and closed her eyes. She wished she hadn't done the last spin before she sat down.

"Here you go." Carter placed a tray in front of her on the table. "I also brought some water and another plate of food. We've been working up and appetite."

Gratefully she drank the water. He was so thoughtful, but looking at the food on the plate made her stomach tighten. Alana took a sip of her wine and sat back in her chair and took some deep breaths.

"I'm good for now." Alana tried to hide a yawn with her hand. "It's been a long day with getting up early for the airport and flying. I think I might be getting tired plus the wine." She held up her glass. "I hate to spoil the party but I think I might go back to the room. I want to make sure I'm rested for all the excitement tomorrow."

"You want me to walk you back to the room to make sure you find it all right?"

"No, no! You stay and have fun." Alana patted his arm with her hand. "I'll find the room. I'll be fine. Enjoy yourself. I don't want to take you away from your friends. You have some catching up to do with Trey"

"If you're sure. I'll come check on you in a while." Carter offered.

"Don't worry about me. I'll be fine. Have a good time. I just need some rest and I'll be fine tomorrow." She stood up and steadied herself against the table. Alana knew better than to drink too much wine. The memory of her bridal shower hangover was coming back.

She made it down the long hallway and up the stairs. Unlocking the door to their room, she kicked off her stilettos and fell down face forward on the bed. She just needed a few minutes of rest and then she would get up and change her clothes. Just a few minutes....

****

The sun shining through the patio doors made Alana stir. Her eyelids felt as if they weighed a ton when she tried to open her eyes. She remembered falling on the bed to rest for a few seconds but nothing after that. How did she get under the cover? She lifted up the cover and checked to see if she was still in the clothes she'd been wearing last night. Her sundress was gone. All she had on was her underwear. She turned her head sideways to see Carter lying next to her on the bed. He was lying on top of the bedding and was covered with the bed scarf.

She carefully slid out of bed and picked up her suitcase so she wouldn't make any noise to wake him. Entering the bathroom, she turned on the shower. She undressed and stepped into the stream of water and showered, trying her best to remember what happened after she came back to the room.

She finished her makeup, dried her hair, and gathered the things she'd spread around the bathroom counter so Carter had room for his things. Alana took one last look in the mirror then opened the door and walked out into the room.

"Good morning." Carter held up a coffee cup. He was standing by the table near the window. His hair was disheveled and he wore only a pair of pajama bottoms.

Alana had never seen him without a shirt. She didn't realize how fit he was. She could tell he worked out. "Good morning." She was finally able to speak. "Is that coffee?"

"The hotel brought us a pot of coffee, some creamer, sugar and everything you need."

"I love this place." Dropping her suitcase at the end of the bed, she joined Carter by the table and poured herself a cup of coffee.

"I thought we could have coffee on the patio." He walked through the open patio doors waving his hand for her to join him. "It's beautiful out here. You can see for miles."

Alana stood by Carter next to the railing of the patio to enjoy the sound of the waves hitting the rocks below them and the seagulls making a musical squeak as they dove for fish in the water.

"Did you sleep okay?" He broke the silence between them.

"Yes." She quickly answered. "What about you?"

"I slept like a baby. I think the wine we drank last night helped and all the dancing and the long flight made me tired." Carter laughed, raising a hand to run it through his hair.

"That could be it." She avoided looking at him, wanting to ask how she ended up in bed minus her dress but afraid of the answer.

"I hope you didn't mind that I had Cynthia come put you in bed. You fell asleep on top of the cover."

Alana closed her eyes and let out a sigh. "So that's how I got undressed and under the cover."

"I couldn't leave you in your dress to sleep so I called Trey and he sent Cynthia down to help me out." Carter explained.

"I feel so much better now." Alana took a sip of her coffee.

"Wait. You thought I undressed you and put you to bed?" Carter turned toward her putting his hand on his chest.

"I wasn't sure." She stared out at the water. "I don't remember anything after I got back to the room." Finally gathering the courage to look at him, Alana continued. "I'm really sorry about what happened. I've never been in a situation like this before and I've never passed out like I did last night. I didn't mean to embarrass you in front of your friends. I mean you had to call your friend's fiancée to come put me to bed." She scrunched up her face, waiting for his reply.

A big hand landed on her arm. "First, you didn't embarrass me. Second, hopefully I'm a good enough friend that you trust me. I'm not the kind of guy who would take advantage of a woman in the shape you were in last night."

"We are good friends and I do trust you." Alana explained. "If I didn't, I wouldn't have come on this trip with you."

"Good. That's settled." Carter turned and began walking toward the patio doors. "Enjoy your coffee and the view. I'm going to shower then we can get something to eat. I thought maybe we could get in some sightseeing before the ceremony tonight."

"That sounds like a plan." Alana took another sip of her coffee and blew out a sigh as she took in the view. Trust was one of the most important traits of a life partner on her grandmother's list. She trusted Carter and he trusted her.

"Oh, one more thing."

"What's that?" Alana turned around to see Carter still standing by the patio doors.

"I hope whoever you marry doesn't mind fighting for their space in bed all night because you're a bed hog." Carter laughed as he walked away.

"I don't...I'm not..." Alana realized he was too far away to hear her. "I'm not a bed hog." She whispered as she turned back to the view.

CHAPTER EIGHTEEN

"I've never seen anywhere so beautiful. Have you?" Alana clung to Carter's arm to keep her balance while she stared around her. They kept walking down the winding walkway toward the piazza.

"I haven't seen anything like this. What's the name of this place?"

"I'll read you the brochure I picked up in the lobby of the hotel." They stopped and she unfolded the paper she was holding in her hand.

"*Sant'Agata (short for Sant'Agata sui Due Golfi) is a pretty hill town between two gulfs: The Bay of Naples with the imposing Mount Vesuvius and the Bay of Salerno with the Li Galli Archipelago. A bit off the coast, this tiny hill town has a great view of Capri as well. Visit the ancient Greek necropolis nearby, and the Monastero del Deserto, a Carmelite monastery that has been attracting travelers with its gorgeous panoramic views since Goethe visited in the late 19th century.*

Just down the road is the fishing village of Nerano, whose beaches sit in the center of the Punta Campanella Natural Marine Reserve. Its rocky seabed and clear waters are a favorite among scuba divers, but be careful; according to Greek mythology, this is where the sirens sang to tempt Ulysses off course. Both Nerano and Sant'Agata are culinary wonders as well. Taste regional specialties like the Sant'Anna tomato and Monti Lattari cheese, or if you want to go hyper-local, don't miss Nerano's legendary spaghetti with zucchini pesto"

"Zucchini pesto. Now that sound delicious." Carter interrupted. "I don't know about you but I'm starving."

"Me too. Let's find somewhere to eat lunch. We can probably just follow the aroma in the air." Alana looked around to see if she could spot a restaurant. Small shops full of pottery and leather goods, and bakeries lined the street. "I'd love to stop and check out the stilettos in one of the stores before we go back."

"We can do that." Carter rubbed the back of his neck as he looked down at her feet. "I don't know how you wear those things without them hurting your feet."

"The same way you wear those cowboy boots which have to be the most uncomfortable looking shoes in the world." Alana pointed to his boots.

"They're very comfortable. We'll have to disagree on that subject."

"Same way we have to disagree on the subject of stilettos. Until I can get you to try on a pair and wear them for a while, you'll never know how comfortable they are," she declared.

"That's not going to happen ever!" Carter exclaimed.

"Fine then." Alana looked at the time on her cell phone. "We do have to watch the time. We want to be back in time to get ready for the wedding."

"I don't know about you but all I have to do it put on my suit and call it good."

She swatted his arm. "Of course, that's all. You're a guy. We women have to style our hair, fix our makeup for nighttime, then stare in the mirror for at least thirty minutes to make sure everything looks perfect. Our dress, our shoes, our accessories."

"I don't think I'll every understand." Carter shook his head. "Why do women go to so much effort when they look just as beautiful when they go natural?"

"I don't know about that. You men don't seem to mind the way we look when we've spent hours on our appearance."

"Saved by a restaurant." He pointed ahead of them to the right side of the piazza. "Let's try this one. This must be the one we've been smelling."

Alana stopped and took hold of Carter's arm stopping him next to her.

"Is this all right? Do you want to keep looking for another restaurant?"

"No. This is fine. I just wanted to say thank you again for bringing me with you. I don't know if I would have ever come here and got to see all this if it wasn't for you." Her eyes teared up as she waved her arm to include everything within eyesight.

"You're welcome, but I should thank you for coming with me. If you hadn't said yes, I wouldn't have come and I would have missed all this." He took her hand and started walking toward the restaurant. "Now, let's go eat before I pass out from hunger."

****

"I don't think I've ever had fresh pasta that good." Carter rubbed his stomach.

"It was delicious. I hope we can come back here before we leave. I spotted a few other dishes on the menu I would like to try." She looked up to see if he agreed.

"Sounds good to me. Are we going to stop at one of these shops before we go back to the hotel?" Carter pointed in the direction of the stores they had passed on their way down the walkway.

"Do you mind?"

"No. That's what we came here for. We wanted to eat pasta and sightsee. I think shopping probably fell in there somewhere." Carter grinned.

"It did with a limit. I mean, I'm stretching my budget to come here. Buying expensive shoes might not fit in that budget, but it doesn't hurt to look."

"No, it doesn't hurt at all." He laughed. "I'm just happy to be here and see everything we have. Not everyone can say they've been to Italy much less eaten fresh pasta with pesto."

"You're right about that."

"Besides, if you find something, you can always try them on, take a card and order them when you have the money. I'm sure they would be happy to ship them to you." Carter suggested.

"I didn't think about that. You're so smart, Carter Owens. I knew we'd make good travel buddies as well as wedding buddies." A smile crossed her face as she took his arm and crossed the piazza making their way to the closest store. He was a good travel buddy. Sharing a hotel room was more than sleeping in the same bed. But he was tidy, didn't leave his clothes on the floor, and cleaned up after himself in the bathroom. She wondered if he was like that at home.

Spotting a pair of white stilettos with rhinestones adorning the edge of the shoe and the heel, Alana was drawn to them. "Look at these. They're amazing. I have to try them on." The clerk motioned for her to take a seat in a chair so she could measure her feet. "I'm a perfect size seven."

"You are in Italy. The measurements are different here." The clerk explained in her best English. "I can convert your size, but I should measure you to make sure."

"Sure. I didn't think of that." Alana took a seat in the chair and removed her shoes.

"I'll find a pair in your size and be right back." The clerk disappeared behind a curtain-covered doorway.

Carter continued looking at the men's shoes while he waited.

"Are you finding anything you like?" Alana asked as she watched him check out several pair.

"Not really anything that's calling my name. They don't have boots."

"Do you wear anything but cowboy boots? I can't remember seeing you in any other kind of shoe."

"I wear sports shoes when I play basketball or work out. Cowboy boots don't look right with shorts and t-shirts." Carter laughed.

"You're right about that." Alana sat up in her chair as the clerk came out of the back room holding a beautifully decorated shoe box.

"I was able to find your size. It's the last pair we have." The clerk sat down on a stool in front of Alana, took her foot and carefully placed a stiletto on each foot. "There you go. They seem to fit perfectly. Why don't you walk around in them and see how they feel?"

Alana stood from her chair and walked slowly to the full-length mirror hanging on the wall. "They're so pretty. I've never seen anything like these." She turned side to side inspecting them from every angle.

Carter walked across the tiny shop. "Those are nice."

"Nice!" Alana exclaimed. "They're gorgeous."

"Okay. They're gorgeous." Carter grinned as he copied her voice. "Where are you planning to wear them? I mean they're really dressy. Is that what you say? Dressy looking? Do they use that term for shoes?"

She met his eyes in the mirror and shook a scolding finger at him. "These aren't just shoes, Carter. These are stilettos and they aren't dressy looking. They are elegant."

"I stand corrected. They're elegant. So where would you wear something so elegant?" Carter waved his hands in the air

"They would be perfect with a wedding dress. One of these days I plan to get married and these shoes are what I imagine myself wearing with my wedding dress." Alana kept turning in each direction to admire the stilettos.

"Are you getting married soon?" The clerk asked as her gaze went back and forth between Alana and Carter.

"Oh, no." Alana exclaimed.

"That's too bad. These are a one-of-a-kind creation by our cordwainer. She made a pair in each size and when they're gone, there will be no more like these."

"Cordwainer?" Alana asked.

"Sorry. Our shoemaker who works with the finest Italian leather." The clerk explained.

"Can I dream about them a little longer? Then I'll take them off. Is that all right?" Disappointment filled her voice. She wasn't in a position to buy them now.

"You enjoy them as long as you want. I'm going to see if I can help your gentleman friend." The clerk stood and walked behind the counter Carter was leaning against.

"Good luck convincing him to try on anything but cowboy boots." Alana whispered as she continued admiring the stilettos on her feet knowing she was going to have to give them up soon.

CHAPTER NINETEEN

The wedding ceremony held at sunset was stunning. Alana was drawn to the view as the couple recited their vows. The water behind them and the waves hitting the rocks on the shore beneath them made the moment magical. She couldn't imagine a more beautiful setting for Trey and Cynthia to begin their life together.

Carter looked handsome standing next to the groom. She was sitting in the second row of chairs behind the bride's and groom's parents and had a perfect view of everyone. Now and then Carter would look her direction and smile.

After the ceremony finished and the bride and groom walked hand and hand down the aisle, Carter joined her by her chair. "Are you ready for some wine and wedding cake?"

Alana noticed how his eyes lit up when he mentioned cake. "I forgot about your wedding cake obsession. Did you sneak a peek to see if you approved?"

"No. I didn't get a chance but I have high hopes. Trey and I always liked the same things." He rubbed his hands together.

"You forget the bride usually has the last say on the cake just like everything else." Alana laughed. "Let's go check it out though and see."

Carter took her hand and led her toward the table holding the food and wine. The bride and groom were at the table and the wedding photographer was taking pictures.

"I hate to disappoint you but I think we have to eat dinner before they cut the cake." Alana watched as Carter bobbed back and forth trying to see the cake. "They're just taking pictures now while the light is good."

"I was hoping for a piece right now." He sighed.

"When you get married, you can be in charge of the order things are done. Cake can come before dinner if you want. Then you can feed the horses. It'll be your wedding." Alana remembered his comment about having a western wedding.

"I'm going to remember that." Carter laughed. "Who wants to wait for cake?"

"Come on, let's go sit down while they finish their pictures. I'll find us a glass of wine." Taking his hand, she led him to the tables, searching the place cards for their names. "Here we are."

A waiter showed up with a tray of glasses filled with wine. Carter took two and handed one to Alana. "Here's to cake."

The rest of the wedding guests had found their place cards and taken their seats at the table. The maid of honor had given her speech and now it was Carter's turn to say a few words. Alana had no idea what he was going to say. Placing her hands in her lap, she turned her face up as he stood and cleared his throat.

"First I want to thank Trey and Cynthia for including me in their wedding. Trey and I promised each other a long time ago we would stand up with the other at our weddings. I'm happy I was able to make that happen. After meeting Cynthia and getting to know her over the past few days, I can see she loves Trey. I also can promise her she's marrying a great man. I've known Trey for a long time and I know he has the qualities of a good partner. He's honest, he's trustworthy, he's loyal and kind and he has a great sense of humor. I'm sure he has made you laugh a lot. He's also a very good friend. I'm happy for you both and Alana and I wish you two nothing but happiness in your future together." He raised his glass in a toast.

Alana smiled as Carter glanced down at her. She was stunned. He'd listed the exact qualities her grandmother had told her to look for. She knew she saw those qualities in Carter. She wondered if he saw them in her.

****

Evening had fallen and the patio was lit by the moonlight and the strings of twinkle lights hanging above. Dinner and cake had been served. The bride and groom had their first dance. The father and the bride had also danced. The couple asked the rest of the bridal party to join them on the dance floor.

Carter stood and held out his hand for Alana to dance with him. He took her in his arms and held her close as they moved around the floor. She snuggled in, enjoying the feeling and wondering if this was what her grandmother missed about dancing.

Being in Italy was a dream. She wondered if the air, the water, the music, the atmosphere added to the closeness between her and Carter. She didn't want to do anything to ruin their friendship but she also didn't want to deny she enjoyed being this close to him, being herself and feeling safe. She never had this feeling with

John. Carter had showed her how to love without even knowing he had.

"What would you like to do tomorrow? We've got a few more days before we leave." Carter whispered in her ear.

"I haven't really thought about it. I was just taking each day at a time." Alana leaned back and looked at him. "Are you sure we have to leave?"

"No, we don't but..."

"I know, we would probably get bored with this beautiful place, right on the water, eating fresh pasta, seafood, pizza, and delicious Italian desserts every day."

"There's that." Carter laughed. "What I was thinking is that neither one of us are independently wealthy so there's work and reality."

"Oh, you're talking about those two nasty things. I guess you're right." She leaned back against his shoulder and sighed dramatically.

"I'm going to pretend I didn't hear that." Carter laughed as he held her closer.

"Let's just enjoy tonight and we'll worry about going home when the time comes. Deal?"

"Deal. Tonight, we eat wedding cake and dance. My two favorite things." Carter smiled as he tightened his arm around her back and dipped her.

"You two make the cutest couple." Alana turned to see Cynthia's mother standing behind her, smiling.

Alana started to explain how she and Carter weren't a couple. They were just good friends, but before she could say anything, Carter squeezed her hand.

"Thank you."

Alana glanced at him; her eyebrows raised. All he did was smile back.

"You remind me of Cynthia and Trey. They were meant for each other. Anyone can see you two are also."

Alana didn't say a word as she watched the woman walk away and join a group of people. She glanced at Carter one more time with a questioning look.

"I want some more cake. How about you?"

Before she knew it, she was standing in the middle of the dance floor, alone, watching Carter pick up a plate from the cake table and take a bite. "What the hell just happened?"

CHAPTER TWENTY

Stepping out of the bathroom, Alana stopped as she saw Carter tossing back the covers of the bed. "What are you doing?"

"I'm protecting myself." He lined a row of pillows down the center of the bed and fluffed them.

"Protecting yourself?" Alana asked. "You seriously don't think you have to protect yourself from me. I'm not going to take advantage of you in the middle of the night."

He glanced over his shoulder. "I'm not afraid of *that*. I'm protecting myself from you taking your half out of the middle of the bed."

"You can't be serious. Those take at least half of the bed. You're not going to have to worry about me driving you off the edge." Alana pointed at the pile of pillows.

"I'm not taking any chances." Carter gestured to the work he had done with a look of accomplishment on his face.

"If you insist." Alana covered her mouth trying not to make fun of him. "I'm tired so I'm going to bed." She laid down on one side of the bed and tossed around pretending to get comfortable.

"I'm not moving them so just find a spot and go to sleep. I'm going to brush my teeth and then I'll be out. Don't touch any of those pillows." Carter pointed to the bed.

"You got it." Waiting until he had disappeared from the room, she scooted the pillows over so she could have more space. "We'll see how he likes that."

****

Waking and adjusting her eyes to the light shining through the patio doors, Alana felt the warmth of a body next to hers. She couldn't feel the pillows Carter had spent at least half an hour positioning perfectly down the middle of the bed. She opened one eye to see she was lying where the pillows had been. There was an arm around her over the bed covers and someone breathing in her ear. She turned her head to make sure it was Carter and to see if he was awake.

She slowly lifted the arm thrown over her and tried to scoot out of the bed without waking him.

"Good morning." Carter whispered.

"Good morning." Alana answered with a questioning tone in her voice.

"I tried to tell you that you were a bed hog, but you didn't believe me." He reached one arm over his head, his muscles flexing, as he stretched and yawned.

"I'm really sorry. I had no idea." Alana sat up on the edge of the bed. "Did you get any sleep?"

"After you settled down from tossing and turning to find the perfect spot, I finally fell asleep." Carter sat up in bed leaning back against the headboard.

"Why don't you go back to sleep. I'm going to take a shower then I'll order us some coffee from room service." She offered as she stood and reached for her suitcase. "It shouldn't take me long.

"That's not a bad idea." He mumbled, sliding back down in the bed and sprawling out to take up all the bed.

"You're so funny, Carter Owens. So funny." Alana rolled her suitcase behind her to the bathroom. "You can get your own coffee."

****

The aroma of coffee hit Alana's senses as she rolled her suitcase out of the bathroom and placed it at the end of the bed. Carter wasn't anywhere in the room but there was a carafe of coffee on a room service cart sitting by the table under the window. She peeked out the patio doors as she poured herself a cup of coffee. He was lounging in one of the chairs on the patio soaking up the morning sun.

"I'm finished in the bathroom if you want it." She took an empty chair on the patio.

"I will in a few minutes. I'm really enjoying the morning air and my first cup of coffee that I got all by myself." Carter glanced at her and smiled.

"I'm really sorry about last night and about the whole coffee thing."

"Don't worry about it." He yawned.

"I hate that you didn't get any sleep because of me."

"I didn't say I didn't get any sleep. Once you found a place to settle, I was able to squeeze in and fall asleep." Carter paused. "I have to admit, it was nice sleeping next to someone all night. I don't think I've sleep so sound in a while."

"I wouldn't get used to it, Carter. This is only for Italy because of the room situation. When we return home and back to reality, you'll be sleeping alone." Sipping her coffee, she tried to read his expression.

He took a drink of his coffee then stood up and disappeared into the room. Sitting back in her chair, she closed her eyes, deciding what to do when she returned home. She knew the trip to Italy, its beauty, the fabulous food, and the different day-to-day living would change her. She'd also experienced a love story between Trey and Cynthia that made her want to find that kind of love for her own life.

"Are you ready to do some more sightseeing?" Carter's voice whispering in her ear woke her.

"I didn't hear you come out of the room." Alana sat up, putting her coffee cup on the table and watching him sit in the chair beside her.

"What were you dreaming about?"

"I was just enjoying the view and thinking about how thankful I am that you asked me to come along with you." She smiled. Not only did he smell good, he was wearing a shirt that made the color of his brown eyes pop.

"I'm glad you're enjoying the trip. I'm having a good time also." Carter reached across and took her hand. "I think we've become better friends while we've been here."

"I agree. We have. It's going to be hard to go back to real life after all this." She waved her free hand around in the air as she stared out into the distance.

"We could stay here the rest of the day or we can go explore some more restaurants. I'm getting hungry." Carter broke the silence. "What do you say?"

"I'd say we check out one of the bakeries that we passed yesterday. I bet we could find something deliciously decadent for breakfast."

"I'm up for that. We can decide what to do next after that." Standing, he picked up the empty coffee cups and waited for her.

Alana followed him through the patio doors closing them behind her. Mixed feeling flowed through her. She did her best to ignore the regretful ones that came with the thought of having to return home soon and embellish the ones telling her she was having the time of her life.

CHAPTER TWENTY-ONE

"There's a bakery around this corner. I can smell it from here." Carter pointed ahead of them.

"I can too. I can't wait to try something absolutely delicious." Alana took a deep breath. "I can smell the butter, sugar, and cinnamon from here. What a great way to wake up."

"Let's go see what they have." Carter moved a little faster making her speed up to stay with him.

"Wait for me." Alana tightened her grip on her bag and walked faster.

He turned around and smiled as he began to jog backwards toward the bakery.

"You're hilarious, Carter." She gave up the race and called, "Save me a pastry."

Walking through the door of the bakery, Alana couldn't believe the choices available. "Oh my."

"Exactly what I thought." Carter waved at the display case. "How do we choose?"

"Maybe we try one of everything." Alana took her time looking at each of the pastries, cookies, and muffins, running her hand along the glass case. She didn't understand all the names but most of them she knew from the way they looked. "I think we've died and gone to heaven."

"There're some tables outside the front of the store. After we decide what to have, we should sit outside and enjoy the view."

"That's a wonderful idea. Now that's settled, how do we decide what to eat?" Alana spotted what she wanted. She pointed to the chocolate croissant and held up one finger. "A cappuccino also, please."

The clerk behind the counter nodded and began filling her order.

Carter pointed to the chocolate croissant and held up one finger then pointed to the orange filled croissant and held up another finger. "A cappuccino also. We're going to have to walk a few miles to work this breakfast off. Then it'll be time for lunch."

"Can we go back to the restaurant we visited yesterday? I saw so many good things on the menu I wanted to try."

"Sure. I'm sure we'll see several more restaurants along the piazza we can try also. I'm open for anything as long as it's pasta or seafood." Carter paid the clerk and picked up their orders on a tray from the counter. "Grazie."

"Follow me little girl. I've got something special for you." Carter moved his head in the direction of the doorway.

"For a croissant, I'll follow you anywhere." Alana took a seat at the table where Carter had placed the tray. She helped him remove everything from the tray then placed it on the empty table next to them.

"What a way to have breakfast. I mean look at this view and smell the air. Pasta and pastry, what more could you ask for." Sitting across from her, he took a deep breath.

She couldn't say anything; her mouth was full of croissant. She nodded and smiled.

Carter held his finger in the air to catch the attention of the clerk who had come to pick up their tray. "*Mi scusi. Puoi farci una foto?*"

"Look at you using your Italian." Alana whispered. "What did you say? I haven't gotten that good yet."

"I asked her if she would take our picture."

Nodding, the clerk took Carter's phone and motioned for them to move closer together. "*Sorridi.*"

"She wants us to move closer and smile." Carter leaned in to the middle of the table.

"You're really good. I'm impressed." Alana smiled and did the same.

"Grazie." Carter laughed.

"*Voi due avrete dei bei bambini.*" The clerk smiled and handed the phone back then disappeared back into the bakery.

"Wait, did I hear bambini? That's baby. Does she think I'm pregnant?" Alana looked down at her stomach in horror. "I haven't had that many croissants."

"No!" Carter exclaimed.

"Then what did she say?"

"She said we were going to have beautiful babies." Carter laughed.

"Oh. Really?" Alana squinted her eyes. "That's the second person who has thought we were a couple. Cynthia's mother mentioned it when we were dancing together. Do we look like a couple?"

"Does it bother you if we do?" Carter locked gazes with her.

"No, not at all." Alana looked down at her plate and tore a piece off her croissant and took a bite.

"Are you sure?"

"I'm positive."

"It seems to me you get a little freaked out when someone mentions it. I mean, last night when Cynthia's mother made her comment, I could see in your eyes you were ready to make sure she understood we were only friends." Carter kept looking at her.

"Is that why you squeezed my hand?"

He didn't answer. He took a drink of his coffee not taking his eyes off hers.

Alana put her hands in her lap and locked Carter's gaze. "It honestly doesn't bother me. I kind of like it."

"So do I." Carter finally answered.

"Good." Alana smiled. "That just leaves one question that needs to be answered."

"What's that?" Carter asked as he took a bite of his croissant.

"How many bambini are we going to have?"

He began to cough, choking on his bite of croissant.

****

"Are you ready?" Carter asked as he returned to their table after slipping inside the bakery.

"I guess so. What's up?" Alana asked as she stood and joined him.

"I saw this hanging on the notice board in the bakery. It looked like a good way to spend the afternoon." He held the flyer for her to read.

"A boat tour? That sounds like fun."

"I asked the clerk about it and she told me where we could sign up. It's not far from here. They leave in a couple of hours."

"Are we dressed for a boat tour?" She brushed her hand down her sundress.

"It says the boat stops in coves so you can swim if you want to. We could go back to the villa and change. We have time." Carter glanced down at his feet. "I don't think I should swim in my boots."

"That's probably a good idea." Alana laughed.

"They serve lunch on the boat and they stop to see the town of Amalfi and the Cathedral of Sant'Andrea. I've heard it's beautiful."

Alana could see how excited Carter was which made her happy. "It sounds like a great way to spend the afternoon."

CHAPTER TWENTY-TWO

"That was a perfect way to spend the day." Alana slipped her shoes off and laid back on their hotel room bed. "I don't think I've ever seen water the color of turquoise. It was so clear and so beautiful."

"I know. I'm so glad we went on the boat tour. Stopping to swim in the coves was probably my favorite part of the day." Carter stretched out on the other side of the bed next to her.

"Mine too. Being able to see the villages with those houses looking like they were tumbling down the cliffsides was amazing." She turned on her side to face him. Doing everything with him was the best part, but she didn't say that.

"We still have several hours left in the day. Would you like to go check out what's happening in the hotel?" He asked. "I think they're having live music on the patio downstairs."

"We can do that. I'll take a quick shower and change then we can go. Maybe find something to eat before we call it a day." Alana picked up her suitcase from the end of the bed and made her way to the bathroom.

"I'll jump in the shower when you're done." Carter called after her before she closed the bathroom door.

Stepping out of the shower, she wrapped her hair in a towel and dried off with another. She slipped on one of the hotel bathrobes hanging on the back of the door and stepped out of the bathroom to tell Carter it was his turn.

"I'm finished in the shower. You can use it now." After waiting a few seconds for a reply and any sign he heard her, she tried again. "Carter, did you hear me?" Still no reply.

Alana walked to the edge of the bed. He had pulled the bedcover over himself and rolled over on his side. He was sound asleep. He looked so comfortable. She hated to wake him. It had been a long, fun-filled day. She was also tired. Maybe they needed to take a short nap and then they could check out what was happening on the patio later.

She laid down on the bed next to him, covered up with the bed cover and closed her eyes.

****

"Are you awake?"

Alana opened her eyes to the sun shining through the patio doors. She rolled over to see Carter standing over her. "What time is it?"

"It's morning." Carter smiled. "I ordered some coffee from room service."

"We must've really been tired yesterday. I don't remember anything after I took a shower." Alana reached up and felt the towel still wrapped around her hair.

"I've already taken a shower and dressed. I thought when you got up we could try something new for breakfast at the bakery we went to yesterday." He walked toward the patio doors.

"I like that idea." She sat up with a frown on her face. "Wait!"

"What?" Carter turned around.

"Today's our last day. We have to leave tomorrow, don't we?"

"That's right."

Alana fell backwards on the bed. "No." She covered her face with the bed covers.

"Come on. Get up." Carter walked toward the bed and reached his hand out for her to take. "Let's enjoy today and worry about leaving tomorrow."

"Fine." Alana took his hand, sat up and threw her legs over the edge of the bed. "I'll get dressed and enjoy today, not worrying about tomorrow. We'll find something to do today to take our minds off having to leave."

"I heard someone on the boat yesterday mention the Path of the Gods. Maybe we should find out about that."

"That sounds interesting. I'll be ready in about thirty minutes." She disappeared into the bathroom, removed the towel from her head and pulled her hair back in a ponytail. After a little makeup, brushing her teeth and slipping on one of the sundresses she had picked from the suitcase before she stepped into the bathroom, she was ready to go.

"Coffee's here." He held up his cup of coffee as she walked out of the bathroom.

"Perfect. Let's drink it on the patio and enjoy the view." Alana suggested.

"I'm way ahead of you. The doors are open and I'm on my way out there." Carter started walking toward the patio doors.

"Wait for me." Alana laughed as she poured herself a cup and followed him trying not to spill.

"I'm going to really miss this." He took a deep breath as he stood at the patio railing.

Taking in the view of the water and the town, she smiled up at him. She had enjoyed getting to know him better these past few days. She would never admit it to him but she was glad the hotel didn't have enough rooms for her to have one of her own. Sharing a room and bed with Carter had brought them closer. If he could put up with her being a bed hog, he could put up with a lot from whoever was lucky enough for him to fall in love with.

"I know. I'm usually drinking my first cup of coffee in the car on the way to work. Being able to step out on a patio with a view this beautiful every morning would be wonderful. I'm adding that to my list of must-dos after I retire."

"We've never talked about what we're going to do when we get older. What are your plans for when you retire? Please don't say you're going to be an old cat lady." They settled into chairs at the table.

"Dang! That's top of my list." Alana laughed. "Well, let's see." She took a sip of her coffee while she thought about her answer. "I hope to have a few grown children with children of their own. I want to be a grandmother like my grandmother. I'm so glad I had her in my life. I miss her. I also hope to have traveled some before I retire, but if there's some place I haven't seen, I'd like to go then. I guess what I really want to do is what we've been doing these past few days. Take things as they come. No plans. Get up in the morning and decide what I'm going to do with my day. *That's* my idea of retirement."

He nodded. "That's my idea of retirement also. I want to do things now while I'm young so when I decide it is the right time to stop working, I can spend my time doing what I want to do. Maybe I'll make stuff out of wood. That seems to be something all men want to do when they retire or write a book about my travels. I don't have to be rich, just comfortable. I also wouldn't mind having a few grandchildren."

"You don't want to go back to your family's farm after you retire? That would be a good place for grandchildren to visit. You could teach them to ride horses and rope cows." Alana smiled.

"That would be fun, but I don't want to return to the family farm to live. Maybe visit. I'll leave that life to my brother and uncles. They enjoy farming more than me. If I want to travel, living on the farm would limit that."

"A book about your travels would be a great idea then. You know, we would make good retirement buddies as well as wedding buddies, don't you think?" Alana asked.

"Yes, we would." Carter took another drink of his coffee. "We also make good travel buddies, but next time we travel together I have one request."

"What's that?" Alana asked.

"Can we get separate beds?"

"You're hilarious Carter Owens. Just hilarious." Alana reached across and slapped him lightly on the arm. "We're going to have to revise your dating profile when we get back to say no bed hogs need contact you."

"Good idea." Carter stood from his chair and motioned for Alana to get up. "Right now, I'm starving. Let's get something to eat at the bakery."

"I'm right behind you." Alana followed him through the patio doors, closed them behind her and finished her last sip of coffee before she placed her cup back on the tray.

CHAPTER TWENTY-THREE

"I found some information in the hotel lobby about the Paths of the Gods." Carter unfolded the flyer he had put in his pocket and placed it on the table next to his coffee and pastry. "Here's what it says."

"If you're in the mood for a hike, set aside a half-day to walk Sentiero degli Dei. This five-mile hike will take you along ancient mule trails, through luscious farmland and quiet valleys, and along the tops of the cliffs overlooking terraced vineyards and lemon groves and the sea. Start from Praiano, or from Bomerano; you'll end near Positano."

"That sound like something I would like to see. I've never seen a lemon grove" Alana smiled as she looked down at his boots. "Are you up for a five-mile hike?"

"What?" Carter protested. "I'll have you know these boots have been on lots of hikes and gone miles around the farm and they did just fine."

Alana raised her arms in the air. "I just wondered if you would be more comfortable in a pair of hiking boots or something with a little more cushion."

"I don't know if I would be throwing stones." He pointed down at her feet.

Sticking her foot out from under the table, she showed off her sneakers as she cleared her throat. "What were you saying about throwing stones?"

"Where are your high heel things you usually wear?" Carter asked.

"My stilettos, you mean?" Alana watched him nod. "When you mentioned the Paths of the Gods, I figured there would be some walking on rough surfaces so I decided to wear my sneakers." She tilted her head wearing a smug smile. "I brought them along, just in case."

"I have to admit that was a smart idea. I wouldn't have wanted to piggy-back you the whole five miles." He laughed as he took a bite of his croissant.

"I'll give you that one. I might have made it half a mile in stilettos and I'm probably being generous. They're definitely not for hiking." She gazed around the piazza. "You want to stop by one of the restaurants or little stores and put together a picnic lunch? We might get hungry doing all that walking."

"That's a good idea. Maybe some prosciutto, cheese, crackers and a bottle of wine." Carter's eyes lit up.

"Maybe throw in some olives."

"Of course." Carter nodded. "We'll probably need to find a tote to carry all this in."

Alana took her tote off the back of her chair holding it up to show to Carter. "I have plenty of room."

"You never cease to amaze me. First your shoes and now your bag." Carter smiled. "You really come prepared."

"Thanks. We should probably pick up a few bottles of water to go along with the wine." She took the last bite of her croissant and a drink of her coffee. "I'm ready when you are."

****

"Look at this view." Alana stood at the wooden railing along the rocky, uneven path. "You can see forever after the morning fog burnt off. Isn't it beautiful?"

"Oh, man. I've never seen anything like it." Placing his hand on the small of her back, he stood next to her as they stared out at the water "You can see the villages we saw from the boat tour yesterday." He pointed off in the distance. "It doesn't look the same from here. A completely different perspective."

"I've never seen anything like this before. It's absolutely beautiful here. The wildflowers in bloom make it so pretty." Alana took a deep breath. She liked being this close to Carter. How easy it was for him to touch her and joke with her. It was as if he was comfortable showing her any kind of comfort or affection. She was going to miss having him to herself when their trip was finished. "It's going to be hard to go home."

"It certainly is. Can you get me one of the bottles of water?" Carter turned his back to her so she could open the tote he'd insisted on carrying.

"Sure." Alana turned and leaned against the wooden railing as she tried to reach in the bag Carter had thrown over his shoulders. Beginning to lose her balance, she reached for Carter to keep from falling backwards. He grabbed her outstretched arms and pulled her forward against him, hugging her tightly. Her heart pounded in her chest. He held her so tight she could feel his heart beating as well. She buried her face in his chest until she caught her breath and whispered. "Thank you."

Placing his fingers under her chin, he lifted her face up toward his. She sensed what was coming next and didn't want to stop him. Carter kissed her, gently at first. His arms still holding her tightly as if afraid he would lose her if he let her go.

Carter finally released her. "Are you all right? You want to finish hiking the path or do you want to go back to the hotel?"

Alana looked around as she took a deep breath. "Let's finish. We've come this far. I would like to see the rest of the path. I promise to stay away from the guardrails."

"That's a good plan." Carter laughed. "Let's keep going."

"Oh wait. You didn't get your water." Alana reached over his shoulder and took one of the bottles from the bag.

Carter took the bottle and shook his head. "I'd forgotten I was even thirsty."

She watched as he removed the lid of the bottle and took a drink. There was no mention of their kiss. Lips that were now drinking from a water bottle had been pressed against hers. And she'd liked it.

****

Carter appeared to be deep in thought. After they returned to the hotel from their hike, she suggested dinner at the restaurant they found on the piazza. She tried to make normal conversation but he seemed distracted. She knew their kiss had to be what was bothering him. She took a deep breath trying to gather up the courage to bring up the subject when he broke the silence.

"You know, we really need to talk about what happened today on the path." Carter stirred his plate of pasta not looking directly at her.

"I was going to suggest that too. It really took me by surprise."

"What do you think we should do about it?"

"I'm really not sure." She paused. "We've been having such a good time on this trip. I really don't want this to make it weird between us. I think we should talk about how we're going to handle it." Alana took a bite of her pasta.

"I didn't mean to make it weird." Carter finally looked her in the eyes. "I saw you falling and I got scared. I guess kissing you was a natural reaction for me to let you know I was relieved you were all right."

Alana put her hand on Carter's. "Thank you for that. I mean for saving me from falling and also for caring about me enough to make sure I was okay."

"You're welcome. Now what do we do about the kiss?"

"Did you enjoy it?" She squinted her eyes as if she was daring him to say no.

"Of course, I did." Carter exclaimed.

"Good. Well, we can't pretend it didn't happen because it did." Alana raised her eyebrows. "We can't pretend we didn't enjoy it because we both did. I guess what we have to decide is whether or not it changed our friendship."

"I don't mind if it changes our friendship for the better. I just don't want it to change it for the worse. Your friendship means a lot to me. We've gotten each other through some tough times these past months." Carter explained.

"As far as I'm concerned it didn't change it for the worse. If anything, I feel closer to you now than before. I *know* you care about me and would do whatever it takes to protect me." Alana leaned in and smiled.

"And I *would* do anything to protect you." Carter agreed.

———

185

"Then I think we've talked about it. We've decided we both enjoyed the kiss. We've also decided we both care about each other. We've decided we both would do whatever it took to protect the other even if I had to rip a few hairs from the head of any woman who tried to hurt you like Kim did."

Carter covered his nose as he tried to keep from snorting out the drink of water he had just taken.

"You don't think I would?" She challenged him.

"Oh, I believe you. I would hate to be that woman."

"What about you? What would you do if another man hurt me like John did?" She waited for his reply.

"I'd do what I had to, making my point that no one is going to hurt you without dealing with me, but..."

"But what?" Alana interrupted. "You don't mean to tell me there's a but?"

"If you would let me finish." Carter held up his hand. "What I was going to say is I don't think there would be much left of any man who tried to hurt you like John did."

"All right. You saved yourself with that reply. You're probably right." Alana agreed.

"Glad that's settled." Carter ran his hand across his forehead pretending to wipe away sweat.

"After all, I've seen you without a shirt on. I know you work out." Alana winked at him.

"I'll take that as a compliment." Carter blushed.

"What about after we go home?" Alana asked. "Do you think it will change our relationship then?"

Carter stirred his pasta. She waited patiently for him to gather his thoughts.

"I guess we have to see when we return home. I would hope it doesn't change anything." Carter finally answered.

"I do too." Alana agreed. "I say we enjoy the rest of the time we have here and then when we get home and settled back into our routine, we take stock again."

"I like that idea. After all, I'm not going anywhere whether we're here or whether we're home. I'll always be there for you when you need me."

Alana's eyes filled with tears as Carter reached across the table and took her hand. She had never felt this close to anyone. *Does your heart normally skip a beat when a friend takes your hand in his? Do you begin breathing faster when a friend looks you in the eyes like Carter was doing now? How do you know when a friend becomes more than a friend?* These were questions Alana knew she needed to find the answers to but those answers could wait until she returned home. Right now, she wanted to spend the rest of the time they had in Italy together just like it was. No pressure. No questions. No reality.

CHAPTER TWENTY-FOUR

Alana rolled her suitcase into her bedroom and fell backwards on her bed. "I'm home." A huge sigh escaped her lips. There was no one here for her to talk to. She was alone after almost of week of having Carter around all the time. She'd never noticed the quiet before. She wondered if Carter was feeling the same.

Exhaustion filled her body. They had stayed up later than they should have, knowing they were flying out early the next morning but missing anything while in Italy was out of the question.

Their last night together was a little difficult. Alana knew both she and Carter weren't looking forward to returning home. They were both trying to enjoy the last of the time they had in Italy before it was gone. After dinner they stopped at the bar in the piazza and listened to live music, enjoying a few glasses of wine and a few dances.

She could tell both of them were avoiding going back to the hotel room. It was going to be difficult sleeping in the same bed together after their kiss on the Path of the Gods. Even though they talked about how it wasn't going to change their relationship, there were still questions.

When they returned to their hotel room, Carter spent time alone on the patio. He told her he was enjoying the view while he could. She wanted to join him, but she felt it was better to give him some time to himself. She changed into her sleepwear and went to bed.

Alana woke every time Carter stirred. She wanted to move closer to him. She wanted to feel the warmth of his body against hers. She wanted him to hold her in his arms like he did on the path. Most of all, she wanted him to kiss her again. That was Italy.

This was reality.

Standing up from her bed, she picked up her suitcase and opened it in the middle of her bed. She tossed everything she had worn in her laundry basket. She placed her pairs of stilettos back on the shelf in her closet. She remembered the conversation she and Carter had at the bakery when she showed him her pair of sneakers. She smiled as she put them back in their place on the shelf.

You have to make room for someone in your life.

Her grandmother's words were as clear as if she was standing next to her. She stepped back and looked at her closet then began rearranging her clothes, opening back up the space she had filled in when she tossed out John's clothing. She made space for someone in her life to fill. She rearranged her shoes on the shelves to leave space there also. She stepped out of her closet and began opening the drawers of her dresser. She emptied out the top drawer on one side for someone to fill.

"There you go Grandmother. I'm making room."
Alana placed her hands on her hips and smiled. Her
stomach began making noises. It had been awhile since
she had eaten anything. It was going to take her some
time to readjust from the seven-hour time difference and
the fifteen-hour flight. Hopefully there was something in
the kitchen. She had been going to the store for only
what she needed before she left for Italy because she
didn't want anything to go to waste while she was gone.

Opening the cupboards, Alana found a box of
cereal. She opened the refrigerator only to see the spot
for milk was empty. "All right then. I guess I get to order
takeout."

Picking up her phone, Alana searched for a
restaurant close that sounded good. After spending
almost a week in Italy and eating the most delicious
fresh pasta, pizza, and desserts, she didn't want to
order anything like that and be disappointed. Her search
was interrupted by a text from Carter.

Are you getting adjusted to being home?

Alana was a little surprised by his text. She
thought he would be getting ready to return to work
tomorrow like she was.

I was just searching through my phone for something to order. I don't seem to have much to eat here.

She sent her text and leaned back against the counter to wait for his reply.

I was doing the same. Cupboards are empty.

Replying with a laughing emoji, she pictured him doing the same thing she was, standing in the middle of his kitchen with all the cupboard doors open. Carter was quick to answer.

You want to meet somewhere? Anything but Italian. Don't want to be disappointed.

She smiled as she sent a text back.

I understand. Was thinking the same. How about a burger? Meet me at Freddy's in 30?

I'll be there.

She found her bag, slipped on a pair of shoes and checked her hair in the mirror.

Walking through the front door of Freddy's, Alana found a table not far from the door so she could catch Carter walking in. She waved when she spotted him enter.

Stopping next to her chair, he leaned down and kissed her on the cheek. "Ciao," he said with a wink.

"I didn't realize how off my eating schedule was until I got home. I usually don't eat this late at night." Carter sat down across from her at the table.

"I understand. I was doing the same you were. I realized I didn't have anything in the apartment. We could always get back on a plane and go back to Italy for a pizza or some pasta." Alana teased, waiting for his reaction.

"I'd love to!" His eyes widened. "I saw you were thinking the same as me. I didn't want to go anywhere Italian and be disappointed."

"Exactly. I think we were spoiled over the past week. We probably need to lay off Italian food for a little while."

"I'm really not looking forward to going back to work tomorrow. Even though I enjoy my job, being off and on our own schedule for a week makes it hard to go back to the grind." Carter scrunched up his nose at the thought.

"I know what you mean," Alana replied.

"It was also really quiet in my apartment. I didn't realize how quiet until I spent the week with you in Italy." His gaze locked with hers.

Alana leaned forward in her chair. "I know. I found the same thing. It never bothered me before to be alone. I enjoyed the peace and quiet, but I really noticed it after we got back." She paused for a second. "But wait. Did you mean that like you missed *me* being around or did you mean I was noisy? Be really careful how you answer." Eyes narrowed, she crossed her arms and sat back waiting for his answer.

Carter laughed. "This is what I missed. Going back and forth with you about something I said. I miss laughing and talking with you is what I meant."

"Good. I like your answer so you can stay and eat with me."

He brushed the back of his hand over his forehead and sighed. "Boy that was close."

"You're hilarious, Carter Owens. Let's get something to eat. I'm starving." Alana began to stand up and make her way to the counter to place her order.

"There is something I wanted to ask you." Carter stopped her.

She turned and sat back down. "Sure, what is it?"

"I thought maybe we could have dinner together this weekend. I thought maybe I would make you dinner at my apartment." He looked at her while waiting for her answer.

"I would like that." Alana didn't have to think about her answer. "I've never been to your apartment and you want to cook for me. I'm impressed."

"It's a date then." Carter stood and waited for her to join him. "Let's order."

CHAPTER TWENTY-FIVE

I'm glad you invited me to dinner." Alana smiled as she took a seat on the couch. "I've been wanting to talk to you." Looking around, she noticed the walls were bare. She wondered if it was a man thing. This was the first time she had been here. He usually came over to her apartment when they got together to talk. Of course, her walls were covered with pictures and artwork she had collected over the years.

She nervously bit her lip, wondering how Carter was going to react when she told him she was falling in love with him. She didn't want to lose him as a friend, but she couldn't deny the feelings she had for him. Feelings that had intensified since their trip to Italy. It had taken her so long to work up the nerve to tell him, but she realized she needed to.

"I'm glad you agreed to come here and let me cook for you." Carter handed her a glass of wine then sat down next to her on his couch.

"Thanks." Alana smiled. "What are we having?"

"A pasta dish I found the recipe for. I've made the sauce. I just have to cook the pasta when we're ready. I thought I would see if it would remind us of our trip. I know it won't be the same, but maybe close." Carter took a drink of his wine. "I've been wanting to talk to you also. I've got something to share with you."

"Hopefully something good. Are you going to ask me to go back to Italy with you?" She couldn't imagine what he had to share. He hadn't given her any idea, but she needed to tell him how she felt. It couldn't wait any longer.

"I wish. No, but I wanted you to be the first to know that I think I've fallen in love." Carter looked directly at her and smiled.

Alana couldn't catch her breath. The smile on his face told her what she was afraid of. He was happy. Her stomach twisted into knots. How could he fall in love and with who? They'd just had a wonderful time together in Italy. How could he have already found someone else?

"Really. You're in love?" Alana couldn't get any other words out after she caught her breath, but they were running through her head. *How? When? Who? Why?* She bit her tongue to keep from spewing the words.

"Yes." Carter leaned forward on the couch putting his elbows on his knees. "It began with confiding in her about what happened with Kim and grew from there. She'd been in a similar situation and needed someone to talk to. She's been trying to deal with the hurt and also trying to learn how to turn it into a growing experience."

"How wonderful. I'm glad she's learning from a bad experience." Faking a smile, she tried to show some concern for this woman who had stolen his heart from her.

"Me too. I realized I was falling for her when watching her deal with her situation helped me through my situation. It's been nice to have a person who let me vent but also helps me find the good in what I was going through. I've learned to laugh again which feels really good. It could've been so much worse. I know that now, thanks to her."

"So, tell me more about this woman. She sounds pretty special." She really didn't want to know any more but it was better than the alternative. It was all Alana could do to keep from screaming *NO! YOU CAN'T BE IN LOVE WITH SOMEONE ELSE!* She picked up her glass of wine and took a sip instead.

"She is pretty special. She's beautiful inside and out. She makes me laugh. She's an animal lover and has the most beautiful green eyes." Carter paused for a minute as he sat back on the couch and looked directly at her.

His face lit up when he talked about this woman. How could he? *What about me? I have green eyes. What's wrong with my green eyes?*

They'd spent so many hours talking about their relationships. They had a mutual bond. Their partners left them for the other's partner. They were wedding buddies and travel buddies for goodness' sake. She'd gotten to know him well enough to know she could spend the rest of her life with him. *Why couldn't he fall in love with her instead of someone else?*

"She sounds very nice. I couldn't be happier for you?" Trying to stop the tears that were blurring her vision from falling down her cheeks, she pretended to sneeze. She had to be happy for him. He would be happy if it were her.

"Bless you," Carter said, reaching out and placing his hand on hers. "I really feel good about it because I believe I can save her from the fate of becoming an old cat lady, traveling alone, sitting at the singles table at other people's weddings and having the bride and groom try to set her up with their single friends. Oh, and falling down the side of a cliff in Italy."

Blinking, she let what he had just said sink in. It couldn't be. *Was it her? Did he save her?* He did save her from falling. Was she the person he was falling in love with? She had to stop her thoughts from racing there without knowing for sure.

"You did what?" She asked.

"She once told me she was going to give up on love and adopt maybe up to ten cats and become an old cat lady. I'm hoping I can save her from that fate. I've realized life can be beautiful if you take a chance." His gaze locked with hers. "What about it? Would you take a chance on me instead of a house full of cats?"

"The woman you're talking about is me? You're falling in love with me?" Alana put her hands on her chest waiting for his reply.

"Yes." Carter smiled. "I'm not sure how you feel about it, but I had to say something. I couldn't let you go on any more dates with losers or attend any more weddings alone or go on any vacations with anyone else but me. I've watched you put your heart out there only to be disappointed every time. I can't let you do that anymore. I don't want you hogging anyone else's bed. I want to be your next and only date and the only person's bed you hog."

"I don't know what to say." Alana took a breath to try and slow her heart rate down. "Except I came here tonight to tell you I've fallen in love with you."

"Are you serious?"

"I am. I've been trying to keep from bursting into tears thinking of you with another woman." She wiped a tear from her eye.

"You have? I've been wanting to tell you, but I wasn't sure how you would react. I decided I would take a chance tonight." Carter smiled.

Alana took his hand in hers. "I'm so glad you did."

"How about we delete our profiles off the dating site and give us a try?" Carter scooted over on the couch closer to her.

Her breath caught as he leaned over and kissed her.

"I really like that idea."

"Me too." Carter took the glass of wine from her and placed it on the table in front of them along with his. He pulled her close to him and kissed her again.

She'd been wanting this since they first kissed in Italy. She'd been wanting *him* since they first kissed in Italy. "You haven't shown me the rest of your apartment." Alana whispered as she placed her forehead against his.

"There's not much else to see except the bathroom and my bedroom."

"Why don't we start with your bedroom." Alana stood up from the couch and waited for Carter.

"Right this way." He took her hand in his and led her down the hallway pulling her close. "I don't have the view we had in Italy."

"I'm not here for the view." Alana wrapped her arms around his neck. Italy was the farthest thing from her mind.

CHAPTER TWENTY-SIX

ONE YEAR LATER

"Wow. You've done some rearranging." Carter entered their apartment living room and placed his backpack on the floor beside the couch.

"I did." Alana stepped back and admired her work. "I've been wanting to make some changes since we moved in. It just didn't work for me the way we had it before." She finished moving the chair where she wanted then turned to look at him. "I hope you don't mind."

"No. It looks great. I know what you mean about not working. I like the chair a lot better in that corner."

"I know we said we would talk about any changes, but I had some free time and it was bothering me." Alana shrugged.

"I also said I trusted you to do the decorating."

"I'm glad because I got a good look at your apartment when we were moving your stuff." Alana grinned.

"I don't know what you mean." Carter pretended to play innocent.

She placed her hands on her hips and glared at him. "Yes, you do. We talked about your bare walls and the lack of color consistency."

"I had consistent colors. It was called what-ever-is-on-sale consistency. Haven't you ever heard of that color?"

"I have now. Thank you for explaining it to me."

Carter sat down on the couch and motioned for Alana to join him. "Come sit with me. There's something I need to ask you." He leaned forward placing his elbows on his knees.

"Sure. What is it?" Alana took a seat next to him, making herself comfortable by pulling her legs under her.

"I know it's been a while since we've been wedding buddies."

Alana interrupted. "Oh, but the last one was the best. I mean we went to the Amalfi Coast in Italy and stayed in that beautiful villa. I don't know if any wedding can top that one."

"This one just might. I was wondering if you would go to another wedding with me." Carter leaned back against the couch and studied her.

"Of course, I will. I hope I'm the only wedding buddy you have now." She tilted her head. "Who's wedding is it? Do I know them?"

"I think so." Carter took her hand in his. "It's our wedding."

"What?" Alana exclaimed as she dropped her legs to the floor and sat up. "Our wedding?"

Carter didn't say anything. He only smiled.

"Carter Owens. Say something. Anything." She watched as he reached in his backpack and pulled out an envelope.

"I went to a travel agency and checked on availability for the same villa where Trey and Cynthia were married. I wondered if you would go back there with me for our wedding."

"You're serious." Alana gasped as she placed her hands over her mouth.

"I'm very serious. That villa is where I knew for sure I was in love with you. That villa is where you and I went to get away from everything and found each other. I would like that villa to be the place where we become man and wife." Carter dropped down on one knee. "I want to know if you will marry me, Alana Andrews."

"Yes, oh yes. I'll marry you." She watched him reach into his backpack and pull out a beautifully decorated shoe box she recognized.

"I remember you telling me that when you got engaged you didn't want a big gaudy diamond that would catch on everything. I thought we could pick out matching bands. So instead, I bought you these." Carter handed her the shoe box.

Alana slowly opened the top and gasped. "Carter, you didn't?"

He nodded. "I saw how much you loved these stilettos the day you tried them on. I had the clerk hold them for me. I called her later and gave her my address and card information and they mailed them to me."

"I can't believe you did this for me." Her eyes filled with tears.

"They looked so beautiful on you and you looked so beautiful wearing them. I wanted you to have them."

"Why?" Alana asked. "We were just friends then. I mean you didn't know we would end up together at the time."

"I think I did. Maybe it was being in Italy with you. Maybe it was us enjoying fresh pasta with pesto together. Maybe it was the way your eyes lit up the first time you saw these stilettos. Maybe it was how close I felt to you when we danced or when we kissed for the first time on the path. I knew." Carter smiled.

She closed her eyes and whispered, "Thank you." Alana was looking at the man she was meant to share her life with. She was able to check off all the traits on her grandmother's list with Carter and know they were true. Her prayer had been answered.

C. DEANNE ROWE

C. Deanne Rowe was born and raised in southwest Oklahoma. She has also lived in Nebraska, Texas, and California. Iowa has been her home for over thirty years where she lives with her husband, two children and their spouses, five grandchildren, and her hero teacup toy poodle, Allie.

She has always loved writing poetry and short stories and became a published romance author later in life. She has published eight books of her own, three in her *Valley* series, four in her *Cowboy Temptation* series and one non-fiction. As one of the Stiletto Girls with Magnolia 'Maggie' Rivers and Glenna West, she is an author of ten novellas in the *Stiletto Girls* series.

You can find additional information about her other writing on her websites:

www.comfortedfromheaven.com

www.cdeannerowe.com

www.thestilettogirls.com

OTHER BOOK IN THE COWBOY TEMPTATION SERIES: